PROMETHEUS UNITES

PROMETHEUS UNITES

THE GREAT INSURRECTION™ BOOK FIVE

DAVID BEERS

MICHAEL ANDERLE

LMBPN

DISRUPTIVE IMAGINATION

Copyright © 2021 LMBPN Publishing
Cover Art by Jake @ J Caleb Design
http://jcalebdesign.com / jcalebdesign@gmail.com
Cover copyright © LMBPN Publishing
A Michael Anderle Production

LMBPN Publishing
PMB 196, 2540 South Maryland Pkwy
Las Vegas, NV 89109

Version 1.00, September 2021
eBook ISBN: 978-1-64971-660-6
Print ISBN: 978-1-64971-661-3

THE PROMETHEUS UNITES TEAM

Thanks to our Beta Readers

Kelly O'Donnell, John Ashmore

Thanks to our JIT Readers

Dave Hicks
Rachel Beckford
Jackey Hankard-Brodie
Angel LaVey
Diane L. Smith

Editor

SkyHunter Editing Team

DEDICATION

For my brother, Danny.

— David

To Family, Friends and
Those Who Love
to Read.
May We All Enjoy Grace
to Live the Life We Are
Called.

— Michael

THE WRITTEN HISTORY OF THE GREAT INSURRECTION

Three months had passed, and life had changed tremendously for all of us.

Our people had a planet to live on, and Prometheus had sent for them.

Prometheus immediately went to work on the board, the laboratories, and understanding the complex economy of this planet as well as the nature of the life that had been made. Not just the gigantes and rocs, but the other life-forms too.

He would deny the term, but for all intents and purposes, he was the ruler. People brought questions to him, and he found the answers.

For those three months, I think it was as close to peace as we ever knew during this entire endeavor, at least for most of us. I could see the itch in Prometheus, the desire to get moving, to find his way back to his wife. He held firm during those months, however, knowing where his duty lay. He had come to a planet and killed their leaders. He had to make things right, or as right as he could.

The universe has a strange arc to it. We had found peace, Faitrin and I, Servia, even the AllMother. The old one who had brought us all together didn't rush anyone. She seemed at home on this strange new planet. She rested a lot, and though she still looked weaker than she had on Pluto, her strength began returning.

The universe, though, wouldn't let us have that peace.

The eyes that had fallen on us decided that it would be better to kill us than let us live in peace. Perhaps those distant warlords knew another warlord when they saw one. They understood that Prometheus wouldn't be sated by this planet, and while they misunderstood his end goal, they saw a war in his future.

So those warlords came to snuff the new warlord out, and our peace ended.

CHAPTER ONE

The planet was a cold one, with snow and ice stretching as far as the eye could see. There were no roads, and anyone who came to this place was forced to travel by air or by animal. It had been cheaper to build transports than roads.

A nondescript one-story building sat in the middle of the tundra. There were no other structures in sight, only the transports that had arrived thirty minutes ago.

There were three main groups of transports on three different sides of the building about a mile away. Some men and women occupied them, while others stood in the snow, wrapped in layers of clothing and holding weapons. No one standing outside the building dared fire on an opposite cohort. To do so would mean destruction for all involved.

Those outside the single-story building waited for the people inside, Two men and one woman. They had not met face to face in ten years, not since the last war that had gone on for far too long. The death toll had finally grown so high that the three warlords were forced to sit down and bargain.

For ten years, their shaky peace had held.

Now, this new warlord—a man from Earth, no less—threatened their peace.

Those on the outside didn't know what was being said. They only hoped that the people inside managed not to kill one another and could somehow find a way to stop the force of nature known as Prometheus.

Cristin de Monaham was thin, and she was from this cold world. Living on a cold world since birth made one hard, or it killed one. There were no other options.

Galer de Brinston was the fattest of the group. A scar stretched down the side of his tan face, and he usually wore his long hair back, not bothering to hide the war trophy.

Simo de Colombus was between the woman and the other man as far as weight. His hair was cropped close to his head, and his eyes were like stones.

Each of the three had one person standing behind them, their second in command. They held different titles for these people, though it amounted to the same thing. The seconds were here to remember what was said and to light a cigar or cigarette if such a thing was requested. In short, they would act as servants and confidants. The position was coveted and only bestowed on one person until their death or retirement.

All six people in this room had been in it ten years previously.

Cristin spoke first. Her voice was naturally soft, sounding much like the cold wind that blew across the wilderness outside. "We all know why we're here. Something has to be done. The question is, how should we deal with him?"

Simo, who was sitting directly across from Cristin, spoke next. He waved his hand like he was swatting a bug as he began. "His quarrel is not with us. It was with that corporation and those monsters they breed. Or the Commonwealth from Earth. Why should this concern me?"

Galer raised his eyebrows. "The monsters they breed? How many gigantes do you have in your service? How many are sitting out there in the snow right now? And don't act like the three of us are without guilt when it comes to selling the monsters."

The two men looked at Cristin. Her business was not as widespread as the others, but it was growing. She bred the creatures to create a solid alternative to what had once been a monopoly.

Simo shook his head. "I was against that business from the start. It still has nothing to do with me."

Cristin's face was a mask of disdain. "If he comes for me, Simo, he'll come for you too. Why stop with my army? Why not free the gigantes you two possess? You're being stubborn right now, and I'm not sure why. You didn't come here to tell the two of us no, so can we stop this charade?"

Simo grew quiet. The woman's words were true. Their

armadas hadn't flown to this world because they thought this man *wasn't* a threat.

"It's a pretty wide opening, especially since he took out the Daxes and their board," Galer said. "He may have halted production there, but we can get it started again fairly quickly. If we go there and end his little rebellion, the bred-for-hire mercenary market would be ours."

Simo spoke again. "His *little rebellion* destroyed the largest mercenary corporation in our galaxy. Underestimate this man at your peril, de Brinston."

The fat man placed his hands on his ample stomach. "I'm not underestimating him. I'm not overestimating us, either. He took out the Daxes by utilizing a glitch in their breeding process. He was stronger than them, and they ended up without the necessary warriors to fight back. That's not going to happen here." He nodded at Cristin. "Her breeding is different, for one thing. Two, our militaries are not based on the gigantes. He won't be able to turn them against us. He won, through luck or strategy, I don't know, but neither of those things will work against us."

He leaned forward on the table, his scar prominent under the bright light.

"He did us a favor by taking out the Daxes. I vote we go there and remove him from power, as he did them." He leaned back in the chair. "We can work out the details about management and profit-sharing later."

Cristin and Galer looked at him.

"I agree," Cristin said.

"And if I don't? What then?"

Galer shrugged, still leaning back in the chair. "Things

remain as they are here, but Cristin and I will go kill this Titan. We'll share the profits of the endeavor."

All three knew what that meant and why Galer had said it. The big man thought the chances of them winning *with* Simo were higher. Perhaps they even needed him. Yet, if they went forward and he didn't, his position would be weakened as the other two gained more credit and power, at least over time.

Simo gave a small nod, knowing that to join them might mean death, but to sit it out would almost certainly mean the same. The Titan might be dangerous, but Galer was right. However he had won, it couldn't be repeated. In some ways, the Daxes had set themselves up to be defeated by creating a primitive creature who would follow any strong man who came along.

The Daxes had thought themselves so intelligent, so high above the crime lords they sold to. They had engineered the creatures and created a legal enterprise, though they'd been nothing more than common criminals. Now they were dead.

"I'm in," Simo told the others.

They nodded.

Planning would come next, but that was just details.

The Titan was as good as dead.

CHAPTER TWO

Warlords were gathering in another galaxy as Alexander de Finita decided his next move. His spies had told him of Kane's newest triumph. The former Titan had gotten himself an army, apparently by destroying the heads of a corporation that de Finita had never heard of. The universe was truly vast, and even the Imperial Ascendant was learning how far humanity had stretched.

He'd kept his empire contained to the Solar System, but he was now wondering if he shouldn't venture out farther once this threat was eliminated.

Alexander had spoken to Caius a few hours before. The old Propraetor was taking Kane seriously, and he was whipping the other Propraetors into fighting shape. Alexander had called a meeting with them for next week. They would all travel to Earth (some were probably already on their way), and he planned on letting them all know the stakes.

The Fathers had called Alexander early this morning; clearly, the same message he'd received had also been delivered to them. The dead bastards were starting to get on his nerves, and he wished more than anything he could simply shut down the whole system. Yes, his forbearers lived inside the artificial intelligence system, and yes, it had helped the Commonwealth rule this Solar System with an iron fist—

But godsdamn, it was annoying.

Perhaps it was petty for an Ascendant to be thinking in such terms, but he couldn't help it. He hated the Fathers right now.

Alexander knew he couldn't shut them down, though. Whatever he might personally think about Kane, he knew his duty, and they weren't wrong. The ex-Titan's strength was growing by the day.

The message Alexander had sent about Kane's wife hadn't worked. It felt like a lifetime ago that they'd had Kane on the dreadnought. Back then, Alexander had felt as if he were somewhat in control of the man.

He had been.

No longer. They couldn't play an offensive game. Now they would have to wait for the ex-Titan to return.

And he would. Alexander held no doubt about that. The Fathers could calculate everything, and Alexander could access their calculations without having to go see them. The man, Kane, was blinded by his love for his wife. There was a ninety-seven percent chance he would return to see her, which to Alexander was insane. He could understand devotion to one's progeny and one's lineage, but to a woman?

It was lunacy.

That madness clarified things for Alexander, though.

The Propraetors were important, but the woman Luna was key. Controlling her was crucial to winning this. It might be the only way now.

Don't be dramatic, the Ascendant told himself. *You sound like the Fathers. He might have an army of half-breed mutants, but you control a star system.*

Alexander was on his way to Luna's room. He'd kept her isolated for the past month, knowing that isolation would cause psychological issues and make her more prone to accept him as her savior. He also wanted to see if she'd talk about what had happened on her own. She hadn't yet, but maybe the isolation would force it.

She'd had contact with her servants, but no one of any importance. To the outside world, the ex-Titan's wife had simply disappeared.

Her father was beginning to cause issues, and the man held some sway on Earth. Nothing the Ascendant couldn't handle, but he knew he'd have to let the woman speak to someone soon.

Yet, the isolation had been necessary.

Because Alexander understood something had happened with the woman, just as something had happened with the Fathers. They had almost demanded that he march down the moment they felt it and question her. Alexander had seen the security video from her room, the one recorded two and a half seconds after the Fathers had their little private conversation.

The Fathers were positive the ex-Titan had somehow managed to travel across space in a way never before seen. They said they'd spoken to the man. Alexander didn't believe it, of course. He'd had the AI run multiple systems checks, but it had detected no abnormalities.

Then there was the security video. The woman had asked who was in her room, shock on her face, trembling and crying.

All of it had made Alexander wonder what had taken place. He still didn't believe what the Fathers told him, and that was why he'd waited before talking to her. Alexander wanted her primed to talk, not to continue the game Luna Kane was so adept at playing.

Alexander wanted to kill her just as he did the Fathers, but he understood that might doom the entire Commonwealth. Right now, she could be used as a pawn, but if she died? It would ignite something in the ex-Titan that nothing in the universe could extinguish. Alexander realized it would be like setting off a supernova right next to Earth.

If he kept her alive, she could still be used.

He reached her door. His body's signature could open it, but he had more decency than to do that to a lady. He waved his hand in front of the panel on the left side of the door and waited for her to check the panel on her side.

After a few moments, the door opened by sliding into the wall.

The Ascendant stepped in. Luna sat with her back to him, a DataTrack open on the table in front of her. He monitored everything that went through the thing, and much of the outside world was blocked from Luna.

As she well knew.

"*Salve*, Luna," the Ascendant said, understanding that her back turned to him was a message in itself.

"*Salve*, Imperial Ascendant," she responded without looking at him. "Am I free to leave the Imperial Residence, or am I a captive here?"

She turned around and faced him. She looked different than she had when she'd first arrived. She'd lost weight, and there were circles beneath her eyes, dark ones that spoke of the little sleep she got at night.

"Would you like to leave, Luna?" Alexander asked. He folded his hands behind his back.

"I'd like to know what is happening and why I've been denied access to my family. I've willingly done what you asked. I've been on board with everything you've asked, my liege, but I'm being treated like a prisoner." She gestured at the DataTrack. "Even the information I'm allowed to see is restricted."

"It's for our safety, Luna."

"Oh, I'm a danger to you now?" She scoffed. "A woman who's never used a weapon in her life?"

The Ascendant made his way to a chair next to one of the windows. He sat and looked outside. The windows in this room couldn't be broken, so the woman wasn't able to throw herself to her death even if she wanted to. Alexander sighed. "You haven't been honest with me, Luna. That's why I've slowly distanced myself from you and left you to your own devices."

"Please, my liege, tell me how I've been dishonest." It wasn't a question but a demand. Perhaps she was done playing the game. Or maybe she would play it on her terms, and the Ascendant would be forced to do something drastic.

"A few months ago, something happened in this room,

Luna." He didn't look at her as he spoke and his voice was mild, as if he were talking about the cloudy weather outside. "I'm sure I don't have to go into detail, but I will, just so there can't be any misunderstanding. I know you're not a stupid woman, Luna. You know that everything that happens within these walls is monitored, tracked, analyzed, and categorized. There's no reason for us to act like that isn't the case. A few months ago, you spoke to an empty room. You said something like, 'Who's there?' and then you began to sob. To shake."

He met her eyes and saw the knowledge on her face. He saw something else, too: fear. Had she thought he hadn't noticed? That something so severe would slip past him? Perhaps she had, given the amount of time that had passed, but that was why he'd done all this.

To soften her up before the blow.

"I want to know two things, Luna, and I want to remind you that it's important you're truthful here. However smart or capable you think you are, I promise you I'm more so. However great your genes are, remember who you're talking to. I say all that because I don't want harm to come to you. First, I want to know what happened. Who were you talking to? Why did you begin to sob and shake? Second, I want to know why you didn't tell me what happened."

He stopped speaking and let silence fill the room.

Something he hadn't expected occurred. Tears filled Luna's eyes. She reached up slowly with her shaking right hand and tried to wipe them away. Her face turned to the floor, and a single tear dropped into her lap. She was quiet as she brought her other hand to her face, trying to stop the tears that wanted to flow.

After a moment, she whispered, "I don't know, and that's not a lie."

Alexander didn't think she was lying. Not knowing and not having an opinion were very different things, however. "What do you *think* happened, then? Was someone in the room with you?" That was what the damn Fathers had said. The ex-Titan had moved across the universe like a ghost, floating from planet to planet and room to room. That was *their* theory.

"You wouldn't believe me if I told you," she whispered, still not looking him in the eyes.

Dear gods, no, Alexander thought. *She can't be about to tell me the same thing.*

What came from his mouth was, "Tell me, and do not lie."

She took her hands away from her face and smiled through the tears. "I thought Alistair was in the room with me. I thought I heard his voice. I didn't tell you because it sounds insane. Even now, I feel crazy saying it aloud." She looked up. "I didn't tell you because it's impossible."

Alexander felt a deep cold settling in his stomach. The Fathers and this bitch had told him the same thing. This Alistair Kane had traveled the universe, breaking the laws of physics, the laws of nature, and no one knew how he did it.

Alexander tried to swallow, but his mouth and throat were dry.

"Has it happened again?" he asked.

She shook her head. The tears had stopped as suddenly

as they'd started. She wiped away those still on her face. "No. Nothing has happened since. I must be losing my mind." She laughed, shrill and slightly crazy.

Alexander stood. "Maybe not." It was time to go to the Fathers.

Caius de Gracilis had done as his Ascendant asked. He had returned to Mars and begun preparing for what might be the Commonwealth's first real test.

He had also begun physically preparing himself for war. He didn't think he would be able to face this Titan down. The Ascendant might call him a former Titan, but Caius believed you could never remove the title. That wasn't the purpose of his training.

Caius simply knew no way to go to war except by leading.

He would fight whatever came to the Commonwealth right beside his men.

Caius had heard about the Titan's newest victory. The man had somehow gotten hold of an entire army, and from the whispers that came to Caius' ears, they were all mutants.

Caius was a student of history, as most men of his stature had to be. The difference between him and the Ascendant was he didn't have the same arrogance. He didn't look at the Commonwealth as a force that couldn't be defeated because his bloodline hadn't started the government. Caius believed it could be defeated since it was only as strong as the people who ruled it.

Just as those who would come for the mantle were only as strong as their leaders.

That was where Caius found himself worrying.

He had assessed the Propraetors and the Ascendant and he'd found them all lacking, at least compared to the Titan, who was quickly turning into a legend.

Had the Commonwealth grown soft over the years? Had the leaders not been challenged enough when training for the position?

Caius understood the answer was yes. It had to be yes. What challenge was there to be had without war? What strife was there with boundless energy being mined?

The Ascendant had fucked up with this Titan and was coming to know strife. He now knew war and loss, and that could either break a man or make him unbreakable. It would appear, from Caius' perspective, that the man wasn't breaking. Perhaps he wasn't even bending.

Caius had kept his grandson a secret from the Solar System. Not that people weren't aware he existed, but they didn't understand the way Caius had raised him. The Titan hadn't seen as far as this threat from outside the Commonwealth, but he did have desires for his lineage. He had always believed that if you had a monarchy, the strongest should hold it. To have a monarchy with a weak leader was simply asking for destruction.

Caius had planned long into the future. His son was to be a politician and his grandson? A warrior.

The plan had been going well until his son died, tragically and accidentally, leaving only the warrior.

Now, though, a politician wasn't needed, but a warrior—and if the Commonwealth survived this coming assault, there wasn't any reason power shouldn't change hands.

Caius had summoned his grandson Hector de Gracilis from the far reaches of Mars a week ago. The grandson was a good man and knew his duty to Mars, the Gracilis name, and his grandfather. He'd finished his job on the other side of the planet and then traveled to his grandfather, which was how it should be.

Now Caius sat in his private dining room, and a servant entered.

"My liege, your grandson has arrived."

Caius stood from the table, his meal mostly untouched. He hadn't known exactly when his grandson would arrive, only having trusted the young man would make it. In his early twenties, Hector was as responsible as any ruler Caius knew. "Please, allow him to enter," he told the servant.

A man that towered over both the servant and Caius stepped into the room. His shoulders were one and a half times wider than Caius,' and he stood a meter taller. One would expect to see red eyes in that massive body, but there was no hint of the color, not even under the most intense inspection. That had been one of the most important pieces of this whole endeavor: ensuring that no red remained in his grandson's eyes.

Caius had made him a mutant as a young man, though he hated the term. He'd hoped his son's political status would be able to reverse the prevailing hatred of mutants, but if not, Caius wasn't taking any chances.

There might be suspicions, but except for the man standing in front of him, every mutant had red irises.

Not this one.

The grandson dropped to one knee and bowed his head. "My liege."

"Stand, stand," Caius said, dropping his hand and taking hold of his grandson's shoulder.

The man stood, and Caius put both hands on his biceps. "You look good, Hector. How are things on the other side of Mars?"

"The rebellion is finished." Small rebellions happened from time to time on all planets—things that had nothing to do with subversives, simply men or women whose eyes were bigger than their stomachs. Hector had a relatively fresh cut running down the side of his neck and continuing below his maroon shirt.

"Were you injured?" Caius asked.

Hector's eyes widened for a second, then he realized what his grandfather meant and smiled. "No, just got a little too frisky in a battle. Barely a flesh wound, Grandfather."

"Come, sit." Caius gestured at the table against the window. Hector nodded, walked over, and sat in the second chair, making everything look small. Caius glanced at the servant, who was still standing at the door. "Please bring my grandson some food."

The servant nodded, obviously having been waiting for the command.

"That's okay, Grandfather—" Hector started.

"Nonsense. You will eat with an old man. I still have a full plate, after all." Caius went to sit with his grandson. "Do you know why I called you here?"

Hector shook his head. "No, sir."

Caius knew his grandson wouldn't lie to him, but he'd been busy killing rebels for the last few months. He knew about strife and danger.

Caius leaned back in his chair and looked at the plate of food. "A true rebellion is coming, Hector. Not like the things we have here on Mars." He tapped his fork absentmindedly with his forefinger. "A rebellion that will threaten us all. Everything. Mars. Earth. Every remaining planet within the Commonwealth's grasp." He put his hand in his lap but didn't look up. "I don't know about the people of the Commonwealth, but those like you and me? The ruling class? We will be killed. Anyone who supports us will also be killed."

His grandson's voice dropped lower. "Does this have to do with Pluto?"

No one with any brains believed the farce the Communications Ministry had put out about Pluto. The Subversives had become too powerful or some nonsense, so an entire planet had to be wiped out of existence.

"Yes," Caius said. "You've heard of the Titan Alistair Kane?"

Hector leaned back in his chair, the wood groaning beneath his muscled bulk. "So that was a lie too? His death?"

A silent nod from his grandfather.

"What would you have me do?" Hector asked.

The food was brought in then, and the two men remained quiet as it was served.

"Thank you, Alfred," Caius said as the man finished up. The servant left, and Hector didn't move to touch his food. Caius continued, ignoring his food as well. "The Ascendant has asked me to call a meeting with the Propraetors. All of them. We're meeting with him in a week. We're going to start preparing then, but until that time, I need you to read up on this Titan Kane."

"Yes, of course, Grandfather," the young man said.

The old man continued, "I want you to be at the meeting. I'd like you to take a new position in our family, Hector. You will be my Consillarius if you'll take the title?"

Most families had the position, and it was an important one. An advisor, a counselor—someone fully trusted who knew all the business of their family's head.

Hector stood from the chair, then dropped to one knee.

"It would be my honor, Grandfather. The greatest of my life."

Caius touched the young man's head. "Your father would be proud of you, Hector. I know I am. In a week, we will have our coming-out party, and then we will decide what to do about this troublesome Titan."

CHAPTER THREE

Fifty years after Aurelius de Finita, the First Imperial Ascendant, rose to power

Nine hundred and fifty years in the past

Aurelius de Finita was a man who understood risk and knew eternal vigilance was the necessary price of power. Someone would always try to take the top spot away. It was human nature and could not be helped. When he thought about the future, it wasn't three months or three years forward. He thought about things in terms of generations. That was why he had started the artificial intelligence project.

He understood he had to worry about his progeny.

Both those who had escaped his grasp and Earth years previously and the young son he had fathered after they left.

He had no optimistic belief that his children wouldn't one day return to Earth and bring peace when they came.

Nor did he think his current son would be ready to rule when the time came. Aurelius was much too old, and someone would try to steal the child's birthright.

That was why he had begun the project, which many had called impossible. They said the science wasn't ready, and it wouldn't be ready until long after he was dead. Aurelius wasn't a man who listened to other's limitations, and he hadn't when he started this project either.

He'd ignored them all.

Now it was nearly at fruition. The artificial intelligence program would be powered on within the next forty-eight hours. In early tests, they'd shown it was possible to upload a human mind without harm to either the AI programming or the mind.

Of course, as with all things great men tried to do, there was now a problem. Aurelius hadn't seen this one coming, though. The people who worked on the project had all been thoroughly vetted—psychologically, physically, in every possible way—and then approved.

At least, that was what was supposed to have happened. If it had, Aurelius wouldn't be standing in front of this locked door, ready to enter and talk to the man threatening to fuck up the entire endeavor. Aurelius was much older now than when his children had abandoned him and the Commonwealth. Twenty years had passed, and he could no longer deny that he was an old man. He still had some of the strength he had once possessed, but much had left him. The only thing that had not left was his will. It was still iron, unbreakable, despite how old he grew.

Aurelius gave a knock and waited for a minute, knowing that the man was inside. When no answer came, he sighed, took a keycard out of his coat pocket, and flashed it across the panel to the right of the door.

The door opened, and Aurelius saw the man he'd come here to talk to sitting in a wooden chair three meters from the door. He was sweating profusely, and he held a weapon of some kind in his hand. Aurelius thought it might be one of the StarBeams that had become so popular lately. His deceased wife had shot him with one two decades previously, before they'd started to be mass-produced.

Aurelius stepped into the apartment, and the door swiftly shut behind him. "Do you know who I am?"

The man's eyes were bloodshot. He was younger than Aurelius by many years and had most likely seen little of this world, let alone the universe. He nodded at the Ascendant.

"Good." Aurelius stepped farther into the room, looking at the furnishings. The young man's name was Renyard, and from what Aurelius had recently learned, he was a genius. The kid had a bright future ahead of him in the Commonwealth. He could have made a contribution.

No longer.

"You have something of mine," Aurelius said. "You stole it from me, and I want it back."

The StarBeam shook in the young man's hand, though the barrel remained pointed at Aurelius. The Ascendant paid it no mind.

"Where's the algorithm?" Aurelius asked the silent Renyard. "Is it here?"

"You're too late."

Aurelius smiled at that and turned to look out the window on his right. "You can put the weapon down,

Renyard. The building has been evacuated. Right now there are at least five weapons aimed at your head, and the moment your finger contracts the tiniest bit, your head will be cracked open like a nut."

He walked over to a small table in front of the window. A picture of an older woman sat on it. The Ascendant knew it was Reynard's mother; he knew everything about the young man. Aurelius picked it up and looked at it for a second before placing it gently back on the table. "There's not much I can do for you, Renyard. Your fate was sealed the moment you decided to take the algorithm, but you're not thinking about the other people you care about. Your mother is still alive and lives only twenty kilometers from here, am I right? You see her every Sunday. She used to make lunch for you, but now you're making it for her because she's not as young as she used to be."

The Ascendant turned and looked at the young man. His face was pale, his hand shaking.

"You ought to be careful with that weapon, the way your hands are shaking. You might accidentally flex your trigger finger a bit too hard, and that'll be the end of everything."

He stepped across the room and took a seat on another chair, this one having much more cushion and a leather back instead of wood.

"Where's the algorithm, Renyard?"

The young man stared at him. A drop of sweat hit his eye, causing him to blink. He quickly reached up and wiped it away. "I don't have it."

Alistair gave a chuckle, more of disbelief than laughter. "We know you copied it. We know you took it. We know it's here. The longer you make me ask these questions, the worse it's going to be for your mom, your sister Andrea, and your cousins. Renyard, I know about them all. I know where they live, and I know where they eat lunch. I might look old and feeble, but looks can be deceiving. Tell me where it is and save them a lot of pain."

Both of them knew what the problem was and why Renyard stealing the algorithm was a massive issue. Aurelius was still in possession of the algorithm, though, so the project wouldn't be stopped. If he died tomorrow, his mind would be uploaded into the AI. That wasn't the problem. The chances of anyone else creating this algorithm were almost nonexistent as well. It had taken decades with the greatest minds working on it. No one could recreate it. No, what mattered was what would happen if someone *else* possessed the algorithm. They could reverse-engineer it. They could even shut down the project, no matter how far in the future it was used. Knowledge of the algorithm gave them godslike power over the entire endeavor.

Aurelius crossed one leg over the other and looked at the floor as he bounced the top leg gently. "If you don't have it, then who does, Renyard?"

"It's off the planet."

This caused Aurelius to look up. Their intelligence report had said nothing about that. "Lie to me again, boy, and I'll take your tongue."

"You want to play like you're one of the g-g-gods," the young man stuttered. "You're not, though. You're just a man, one who is crueler than most others. That's the difference. That's how you've made it so high up and kept everyone else so far down. Without the algorithm, your power isn't almighty, and you know it. I don't have the algorithm anymore. I've made sure it's not here, not on this planet, and one day, it won't be in this Solar System either. Your chance at godhood is gone, Imperial Ascendant."

Aurelius stared at him, his anger raw on his face. He didn't need to put the kid in a truth chamber to know he was telling the truth. He'd somehow done what he'd said he'd done. It was almost impossible for Aurelius to believe the algorithm was out of his grasp.

"You made a mistake that you don't yet fathom, boy," Aurelius said. "I promise you, though, you're going to understand it very well before you quit drawing breath." The Ascendant was quiet for a moment, staring at the man who had jeopardized everything. He didn't understand how someone like him had taken decades of planning and thrown it all into the wind. "Where did you send the algorithm?"

Renyard put the StarBeam on his lap, releasing his hold on it. He was likely to accept his fate, but Aurelius didn't like the look on his face. The fear that'd been there when Aurelius entered was gone, replaced by something close to peace.

He looked at the weapon and gave a very small smile as he spoke. "I suppose I can tell you now because it doesn't matter anymore. There's nothing you can do to stop it." He looked up at the Ascendant, and there was madness in his eyes. Pure, unadulterated madness, because who could say that to the Ascendant and not be insane? "The algorithm is in a ship that's already left Earth. I won't tell you which ship or where it's heading, though you'll probably try to get it out of me. That's fine.

If you do, it won't matter anyway. Right now, the ship and its AI will do nothing with the algorithm. However, the moment before the AI is destroyed, it's going to send the algorithm to two other ships. That same process will replicate itself over and over, multiplying the number of places the algorithm is stored. The only way you can keep it from getting into multiple hands is by doing nothing, my liege."

The last two words were nearly spat.

Aurelius stared at the young man for a long time. He didn't doubt what he'd said was true, though they would find out for sure in a short time.

"I only have one question for you, Renyard. Was it worth it?"

Still smiling, he said, "Yes. In the end, it will be."

The Ascendant looked down and smirked. "The problem with endings is that there are so many of them. There is my ending, the Commonwealth's ending, and what will come before both of those—your ending. Shortly, you're going to feel very different about the end and worth." He looked up. "I promise that."

Renyard never got the chance to tell the Ascendant who was right, but his screams did lend credence to the idea that he might have been wrong.

Present Day

Life had changed in ways Ares hadn't understood were possible.

Perhaps the greatest change was trying not to think of

himself as Ares but Romulus. For a long time, he'd been called by his callsign, and now it most likely was disgraced.

He couldn't know.

More, the change of his name was now the least of his worries.

Especially at this moment.

"FUCKING GODS, VEENA! I THOUGHT THEY USED TO CALL YOU HAWK!"

"Go to hades, Ares!" she shouted at him as she pulled the ship up.

Ares was strapped in, his back to Veena, looking out the panels in front of him. A laser had just taken off one of his lasers outside the ship, which meant he was only operating with four now.

"It was your damned idea to get this piece of shit!" Veena shouted from behind him.

This is true, he thought as he aimed the lasers. The AI on the ship had turned out to be worthless when it came to defense—and flying—so Ares was now on defense and Veena was flying the damned thing.

While pirates chased them.

Ares pulled the trigger in his hand and watched as one of the corvettes burst into flames, spun out of control, and quickly burned out.

Ares' muscles tensed. His training kept him from screaming a wild "YES!" but damn, that felt good.

Because they were surely going to die.

The ship was relatively upside-down, its artificial gravity telling them their feet were now up.

"Nice shooting," Veena remarked. "Only four left."

Yeah, they were going to die.

"Hold on," the former Fleet Primus said, then banked hard to her left.

Ares' eyes widened as he realized Veena's genius. It was a superb move; before him for mere seconds were all four pirates.

Ares' genius clicked into action then, his reflexes taking over. Four pulls of the trigger and the ships were all infernos, those inside dead or dying.

He relaxed in his chair, the adrenaline draining from his body. "Nice flying."

Veena laughed behind him. "Nice shooting, Ace."

It was a nickname she'd given him, and he hated it.

She righted the ship, and both unstrapped from their seats. They'd been able to get away from the main pirate ship with ease, but the corvettes had caught up with them, their ships far superior to the one they now had.

It was worse than the previous one, which Ares had decided to give up, and Veena had reluctantly agreed.

"How much fuel do we have, Ralph?" That was the name Veena had given the AI.

"You'll need to find a refueling station in a hundred and twenty-four hours unless you plan on stealing from more pirates. Then it will most likely diminish quite a bit."

"How far away is the nearest refueling station?" she asked.

"One hundred and twenty-five hours."

Ares sank deeper into his chair. "Can you stretch it to get us there?"

"Yeah," the AI answered. "It won't be pretty, though."

Ares stood up and left the bridge. He knew Veena was

angry about changing the ship, but the cargo they now had was worth two of the previous ship.

She wasn't keen on stealing from pirates either, but there weren't a lot of job openings for Commonwealth criminals. Even out here in the far reaches of this galaxy, there would be spies and bounty hunters looking for them. Ares had no idea how many people would be hunting them. What he did know was that a bounty existed.

He didn't think they would live much longer, but they'd survived another gunfight, and not much else mattered at the moment.

It'd been his idea to raid the pirate ship, and although Veena had protested, she knew they needed the loot they had acquired.

It was a rumor. A myth. Something Ares had heard about in the Institute but no one believed existed. How could it?

The story was simple, but there'd never been any proof. Back at the Institute, very few people whispered of it, and when they did, it was done in the most private places. If you were caught talking about a rumor like that, you'd most likely be removed from the Institute. Ares has asked his father about it only once, and the man had said, "Just rumors made up by people who weren't strong enough to defeat the Ascendant. Don't fill your head with those things, and don't let anyone hear you mention it again."

Ares had followed that advice until a few months previously. He'd heard the rumor again, but this time on a planet far from Earth and the Commonwealth.

The argument with Veena had been brief but powerful.

It came to this: if it was true, what would it be worth? It

could buy them new lives. It could hide them from the Commonwealth forever. With that kind of money came abilities they couldn't even fathom right now.

After the first Imperial Ascendant had united Earth, his regime had gone unchallenged for a long time. It seemed as if peace would reign forever since that was before the Subversives had begun their long-lived revolution.

Ares didn't know the exact timeline. He doubted anyone alive did, and really, it wasn't important.

A man had said the Imperial Ascendant was creating an artificial intelligence unlike any ever dreamed of. The AI would allow the Ascendant to upload himself into it, as well as any future Ascendants. In effect, it would create a knowledge base unlike any ever amassed and give the Ascendant's lineage an edge on controlling humanity.

This man couldn't stop it from happening. He didn't have the power, the knowledge, or the skill. The rumor said he had something more important, though; he had the algorithm. Ares didn't know much about algorithms, computer science, or anything that had to do with technology, but he did understand the rumor. The algorithm would supposedly allow its possessor to shut down this mythical AI. Or create another one.

What mattered to Ares—especially this far out in a cold, vast universe—was the power it would give him. He had no dreams of returning to the Commonwealth with the algorithm, but it was clear that whoever had it now didn't understand what it could do. They didn't understand its importance. Ares did.

He left Veena in the front of the ship. She'd gone along with his plan, but she still showed little interest in it. Now, though, the thing was nearly in his hands. He walked to the cargo bay where he'd thrown the piece of luggage before rushing toward the defense seat.

He entered the bay and stopped about five meters in front of the box. It was a small thing, not even a meter wide or tall. It was obviously old, the metal covering the outside chipped and scratched.

Truthfully, Ares didn't know what he would do with it if he possessed it. Even now, standing in front of the box, he wasn't sure he hadn't gone on a fool's errand. His life had degraded so far that he would chase almost any hope, no matter how small the chance it might help him.

"Enough," he whispered to himself. "See what's in the damned thing."

He crossed the few meters and picked up the box. There were locks on the thing, but it had obviously been made in a much less secure time. Ares used a laser pen to slice through the multiple metal locks.

He sat on the floor as he opened it in between his legs.

A clear glass tube on a foam casing. Ares picked up the tube and saw a screw-on top. He quickly twirled the top to the left and opened the glass container. He probably should have been worried about poisonous gas or an explosion from the case, but he'd ignored all those considerations. Ares figured he should have been dead by now, and if an ancient case killed him, it was the will of the gods.

No explosion or poisonous gas. Rather, he found a single sheet of paper inside the glass tube. It was old and brittle. Something inside the box or glass had kept it from disintegrating, and Ares knew he'd need to get the sheet copied or protected soon. The thing might just fall apart from advanced age.

He read the piece of paper. He couldn't help himself.

If you're reading this, you're in search of the algorithm. I don't know what year it is or what has happened since I took the algorithm and gave it to the universe. I am most likely dead at this point, and my name isn't important anyway.

What is important is the algorithm, and that's why I've set it up like this.

First, a few things: the algorithm does exist. It is not a lie.

The AI and the ability to upload a human mind into a digital cloud also exist.

A single copy of the algorithm was made at some point in the past, then uploaded into an artificial intelligence in a ship that was destined for elsewhere in the universe.

If the AI was going to be destroyed, its programming determined that it had to send the algorithm to two other ships that were predetermined. The programming would replicate, and more destruction to the AI would result in another two messages, and so on.

What you're now holding is the direction to that first ship. If it still exists, the algorithm will be on it. If it does not exist, the algorithm has started to spread, and this paper is most likely unnecessary. Give the numbers at the bottom of this page to any ship with an AI presence, and you'll be on your way to the algorithm—or at least to where it once resided.

If you've found this, you know my reasoning for stealing it from the Ascendant, and perhaps yours aligns with it.

I have faith that not all of mankind is like the Common-wealth's first Imperial Ascendant. I have faith that others who find this won't try to recreate it but will do the right thing. The noble thing.

They'll destroy it.

Ares finished the short letter and glanced at the twenty-five digits at the bottom of the page.

He didn't know what it all meant, only that it wasn't making a ton of sense. He spent a few minutes sitting by himself, thinking about the letter and the ancient and apparently unopened box, then decided he needed to talk to Veena about it.

She had disagreed with the endeavor, and this would probably only piss her off more. However, she might be a lot of things, but stupid wasn't one of them. Ares placed the letter back in the tube and sealed it with the screw-on top. He watched in amazement as the top shot gas into the tube, a vapor that quickly disappeared but was obvious in its purpose. The letter had been preserved by this casing. That gas kept it from deteriorating. Ares would still need to make a copy of it as quickly as possible, but he felt a little bit better knowing if it was in there, it would be relatively safe.

He closed the box and walked quickly back to the front of the ship.

Veena was still in the pilot's chair. She didn't look at him as he entered the small room, just said, "Did you find what you were looking for? I hope so because this ship is worse than I thought."

He placed the box in her lap.

She stared at it. "What's this?"

"Open it and see. Just be careful. What you're about to look at is older than either of us ever imagined."

Veena did as he instructed, taking her time pulling the tube out and the paper from it. She read it quickly, just as he'd done, then stared at the digits written on the bottom.

"It's real, Veena," Ares said. "I didn't think it was either when we went after that pirate ship, but hades, it was better than what we were currently doing. That letter proves it's real, though."

She didn't shake her head, but her eyes narrowed as she stared at the sheet. "You had to open the box, didn't you? I see the laser burns on the locks. Why hasn't it been opened before?"

Ares shrugged, though his voice was excited. "I have no idea. Maybe those pirates didn't know what they had. Maybe it has been opened but was repaired. A dozen different things could have happened, and when we get to a more powerful AI, we can probably see if the box has been opened and repaired. The rumor was real, though, Veena. Maybe the AI on this ship can scan it and give us a time it came from. It's ancient, though, and you know it."

"What are you proposing we do, Ares?" she asked quietly. "Do you want to put the coordinates in and rush off to some ship that cannot possibly exist, given how old it would be?"

Ares grabbed the gunner's seat and pulled it around so he

faced Veena, then sat in it and leaned forward. "It exists, Veena. Think this through. If it'd been destroyed, you would have had two copies of the algorithm out there, and eventually, something would have happened to at least one of those ships, if not both. That would put it at four. The chances of *those* ships making it for a thousand years is almost zero. The algorithm would be in almost every AI that exists right now if that first ship hadn't survived. That's the simple math of it."

Veena finally shook her head. "No. The chance of that first AI existing for a thousand years is zero."

"Then where are the copies of the algorithm?" Ares asked.

Veena looked up, her eyes narrowed and a smirk on her face. "It's all a lie. The algorithm isn't real. This is a forgery. The ship never existed. It's a galactic practical joke."

"What if it's not?" Ares felt alive for the first time in a long time. He'd felt the dimmest bit of hope when they'd set off after that pirate ship, but now, given the letter on Veena's lap, he felt like they had a shot. At what, he wasn't sure, but something other than running and facing the very real danger of starvation.

"I want to think about it," she whispered as her eyes dropped back to the letter. "I want to refuel this ship, try to get another one, and get a night's rest after that. Then we can talk about this again. I'm not making any decisions right now."

"That's fine," Ares agreed.

He knew Veena was more conservative than he was, but he also knew she had once been a Primus. You didn't get to that spot by hiding from danger or refusing to risk your life for something great.

They had landed the ship and begun the refueling process. Veena had hardly spoken to Ares when they dropped the ship off. Most ships used either an advanced nuclear or a deFinita-189 drive, both of which negated the need to refuel. This thing had been built cheaply and was intended to be sold cheaply. There honestly weren't many refueling stations around anymore, and the ones that did exist weren't places you wanted to hang out for a long time. Cheap things brought cheap people, and many of them were cutthroats.

Veena was angry at him about this ship, and he'd let her be. He'd spent his time verifying the age of the letter as well as making a digital copy of it. The letter dated to the time of the first Imperial Ascendant, which was exactly what Ares had wanted to hear. He'd left the verification information on Veena's DataTrack so she'd see it in her own time.

He also got the box scanned. It wasn't as old as the letter, so it couldn't be the original transportation case. The scan also told him the locks he'd burned through with a laser had been meant for personnel keys; the box read a person's signature and would only open for certain people.

It was a cheap thing, about a hundred years old. That meant whoever had built it had known about the possibility of the locks being easily foiled but hadn't cared or hadn't had the money to fortify it. That didn't make a lot of sense to Ares, especially not for something this important.

Veena spent her time searching for another ship while the refueling process continued. She radioed him at one point, letting him know she'd found one, but it was going to pretty much exhaust their finances. It had hoverblades in it, transports kind of like a motorbike, that might come in useful for any land travel they encountered. Even so, it didn't come to much.

He said the decision was up to her and went on thinking more about the algorithm.

They'd rented a single room with two beds in a rundown building, though everything on this refueling station was rundown. He'd tried putting the numbers from the letter into a simulator, but only an error came back. Ares wasn't advanced enough in spaceflight to know all the different reasons that could be, so he tried other ways of finding out where the number might lead. His efforts came to nothing.

Finally, a little after standard midnight, Veena came into the room.

She sat on the foot of her bed and was quiet for a few minutes. "I haven't decided what to do about the ship yet. If we buy it, we're pretty much going to have to turn into pirates ourselves or pin all our hopes on this algorithm of yours. Even if we find it, I'm not entirely sure what we'd be able to do with it. That's a big if because I still don't think it exists."

Ares said nothing. He knew she was thinking aloud.

"The numbers aren't going to work unless we put them into a ship-based AI," she continued. "I checked it with a simulator, and nothing came back. The original programmer was intelligent in a way few space navigators are. The digits were created to bypass simulators so someone can't sit on a planet and figure out where the algorithm is. The creator made it so we have to go there. I'm fairly certain that even when we put it into an AI, it won't be able to tell us the final location. It'll feed us piecemeal information on how to get there."

Veena stopped talking for a few seconds and gave a long sigh, then shrugged and chuckled.

"I don't know what I thought we'd do when we got out here. I only knew I couldn't follow the Imperial Ascendant anymore. I know piracy is just about the most dishonorable thing I can think of, so that's pretty much out for me. I ran some numbers, and if we get the new ship, we can purchase enough supplies to last us a month. After that, we're dead broke. If we go after this algorithm, we're going to need a ship that doesn't have to refuel because we won't be able to afford it again." She turned and looked at him. "Do you expect either of us to have a long life?"

Solemnly, he shook his head.

"Me either. Most likely, the algorithm doesn't exist, and if it does, I don't think it's just floating around on a dead ship in space. I think we'll be putting ourselves in a lot more danger going after it."

"Agreed."

Another large sigh came from Veena's chest. "Fuck it. Without the Commonwealth's missions, space is pretty damn boring. I don't think I want to live a long time out here anyway. Let's go find this algorithm."

CHAPTER FOUR

Alistair lay in his bed, not wanting to get up. The planet's star, which he always thought of as the sun—hadn't yet come up over the horizon, and darkness still reigned. His eyes were closed, and he saw Luna in the blackness.

He hadn't visited her again with his mind, and he wasn't sure he wanted to. He understood how badly he'd scared her, not meaning to.

Alistair would get up soon; he had to. He wasn't sure he regretted the decision to come to this world, but it was close. He hadn't understood the complexities of reversing a hundred years of culture and breeding. He hadn't understood how *hard* it would be, though he did now.

In some ways, it gave him a new respect for the Commonwealth and the Imperial Ascendants. Alistair could hardly fathom what those men had done for the past thousand years, especially now that he'd done it for a few months.

His time here was coming to a close, though, and he was ready. Whatever ended up happening with this insurrection, he now knew he would never rule. He would reject the mantle regardless of who asked him to do it.

He allowed himself to smile in the darkness.

Thinking so far into the future was a fool's game. He had accomplished more than he ever dreamed of, but they still weren't anywhere near their end goal. Despite everything he'd done, he most likely would not live to see Earth again.

Yet, he had to keep waking up and making progress toward his home.

He sighed and opened his eyes, and Luna's face disappeared. He swung his legs off the bed, and the lights turned on in the room. He squinted his eyes for a moment but stood and made his way to the bathroom.

His first meeting was with the AllMother. It wasn't one he wanted to have because she refused to participate in strategy, yet he had to talk to her.

He finished getting ready, but the sun still wasn't up when he left his room. Alistair was gaining more control of his mind, though it still largely remained a mystery to him. He was coming to understand that he only gained more control when he was forced to. When the world put him in positions where he could either die or adapt, he adapted. At the top of the tower, he'd done something that ten minutes before would have been impossible for him, killing the gigante with his Whip while keeping Dax Junior's trigger finger from moving.

Over the past three months, Alistair had been practicing, though if he was honest with himself, it frightened him. He didn't want these powers, and he had no idea how dangerous they might be. However, he knew he needed them if they were going to have the smallest chance.

So he practiced, just as he did with his body. He was now able to move things with different weights from different ranges. At first, he had only been able to do it with his eyes closed, but now he could keep them open.

He'd designed a test that he was going to put himself through in the next couple of days since he wanted to see how strong he'd become.

Or hadn't, depending on the result of the test.

Alistair walked to the AllMother's room. The entire group lived within one compound, the same one much of the previous board had lived in. The planet's culture was so different from Earth's that it was hard to believe the people who'd lived here were human. Their lives had been dedicated to the breeding of gigantes and entire families lived in one place. It was more like the pre-Commonwealth cults Alistair had heard about.

Alistair reached the AllMother's room and had to smile when he saw her door was open. She'd known he was coming.

Alistair stepped into the room and found the AllMother lying on a couch on the far side. Her eyes were closed, though she said, "*Ave*, Prometheus."

"I'm not sure I've heard you say that before," Alistair remarked as the door closed behind him.

"I guess an old drathe *can* learn new tricks."

Alistair was used to her using expressions he didn't understand. "That something from before my time?"

The AllMother still didn't open her eyes. "Well, you

replace 'drathe' with 'dog' and a few more words have to change, but yes."

Alistair crossed the room and sat in a chair next to the AllMother's feet, then said, "Expecting me? I think your abilities might be a bit stronger than you let on."

She gave a small smile. "It doesn't take a lot of ability to know when my leader wants to speak."

"Yeah?"

"Sure. You have a tell, Alistair."

He raised an eyebrow. "What is it?"

"Obs. He doesn't eat like normal. You only want to speak when something is bothering you, and Obs can tell that as well as anyone. I've had that door open for the past three days at this time, wondering when you were going to show up."

The old woman was observant, but Alistair wasn't buying that was *all* of what had been in play. He'd seen her kill three Myrmidons without raising a hand. "Do you know what I'm going to ask?"

Her smirk remained on her face. "Maybe, but I'm going to make you say it."

He leaned back in the chair and sighed. "Anyone ever told you that you can be really annoying?"

"No, child. I can kill people with my mind. That usually helps them remain civil. Now, why did you come so early?"

Alistair looked at the window. It was still dark, and he liked that. To be up before the world—there was something elitist about it. "I don't know what to do next, but I know we can't stay here forever. I'm not going to govern this planet. I'm going to go get my wife back, but I don't know how. We're not large enough, not by a long shot. I need advice. I need to know what you think, and I know you've resisted any and all entreaties on my part to give me anything." Staring out the window, he said the only thing that came to him. "I'm lost. I can't go conquer world after world until I have an army big enough to defeat them."

He stopped talking and didn't look at her. He kept his eyes on the darkness, knowing what would come next: her saying she didn't know what to do either.

"You ever heard of a people called Native Americans?" the AllMother asked. "Or maybe you've heard the term 'Indians?'"

Alistair turned his attention to her, shaking his head. "No."

"They're gone from the universe now, but they were an ancient people that pre-dated what ended up being America, which pre-dated my father. They grouped themselves by what they called tribes, or that's the closest translation I know for it. One of the tribes had a saying, and while it's not completely apt, you may understand its meaning. It was 'Sometimes I go about in pity for myself, and all the while, a great wind carries me across the sky.' I don't think you're feeling pity for yourself, but you still don't understand your destiny. You can only stay here so long, Alistair, despite what *you* want. Eventually, the wind is going to pick you up and carry you back to Earth. That wind is so strong that anyone around you will be pulled back too."

Alistair thought about what she'd said for a moment. "How does that help me, AllMother? What are you telling me to do? Look up at the sky and wait for it to come?"

His anger was rising, or perhaps something closer to

frustration. Maybe a mixture. He didn't need old sayings from dead people, he needed something concrete.

The old woman opened her eyes and slowly stood up from the couch. She faced Alistair. "I think you know by now, Alistair, that everything I do is to prepare you for when the wind drops you back off. Nothing else matters to me. If you consider me a fool, then I chose wrong, but I know that's not the truth. Should you look up at the sky? That's exactly what I think you should do."

The two stared at each other for a few moments, neither saying anything.

Finally, Alistair leaned forward, elbows on knees, and nodded. "Okay, then." He stood up and walked out of the room. Obs was waiting for him at the other end of the hall. When they'd first gotten here, the drathe had woken up at the same time as Alistair and followed him everywhere. As he'd gotten more comfortable, he'd started sleeping in, having no desire to wake up at the ungodly hour Alistair did.

"You could have come in," Alistair said as he reached the animal. "She gave me about as much information as you would if I'd asked you the question."

The drathe nipped the air near his hand as he turned the corner.

There was more to do today. More than Alistair wanted to consider, and what the AllMother had given him was the same as getting nothing. Was he supposed to go outside and look up at the clouds? The old woman had put fire in his blood with her refusal to give advice.

Alistair knew Thoreaux was up. He was a shockingly good administrator. Alistair thought that if they ever won this thing, Thoreaux would fit in well inside a government. He had the knack for it, unlike Alistair.

He and Obs walked through the compound until they reached Thoreaux's room. Alistair gave a knock, and the door opened a moment later. The rooms were like luxury apartments with everything one might need in them. Alistair saw the kitchen light on and headed through the living room toward it.

Thoreaux was on one side of the table, Faitrin on the other. Both had DataTracks open and were pouring over reports. The two were partners and lovers, and they worked well as a team, which was good because Alistair couldn't afford quarrels among his council right now.

Faitrin looked up from the table. "How are things?"

Obs trotted over to her, and she scratched behind his ears for a few seconds.

Alistair pulled out the third chair and sat. Obs curled up under the table and closed his eyes, clearly glad to be able to sleep again. "They've been better, but I suppose they've been worse too. Thoreaux, I need your opinion on the nonsense the AllMother just told me."

Thoreaux looked up from the DataTrack and leaned back in the chair with an eyebrow raised. "This should be good. Let's hear it."

Alistair gave them a shortened version of the already-short conversation, ending with her telling him to look up at the sky. "I've got to talk to Caesar about his work with the gigantes today because it's not easy explaining to thousands of them that they don't have to follow whoever kills the most people. I've got to deal with Relm and the issues with trying to start some kind of commerce besides the transfer of species. I've got a lot to do, and deciphering what the hell she's talking about isn't on the top of that list, though it sort of needs to be."

"So," Thoreaux said, "we're leaving?"

Alistair chuckled. "Sure, as soon as this wind picks us up and starts carrying us because right now, I don't know where to go." He paused and tilted his head to look at the ceiling. "Still, I know she's not lying to me. There's truth in what she's saying. I just don't know how to figure it out."

Thoreaux's lips drew into a line and he looked at Faitrin. "You got any idea what it means?"

"Ha." Faitrin shook her head and smiled. "I've known the woman for less than a year. You've known her your whole life. I don't know what she's talking about."

Thoreaux shook his head, glancing away. "I mean, I don't know. She's not telling you to literally go look at the sky, but…" He looked up with a light in his eyes. "It sounds like something is going on above us."

"What does that mean?" Alistair's frustration was returning. "There's a lot of universe out there, and I'm not sure how I'm supposed to scan the whole thing."

Thoreaux shrugged. "You're the leader, Pro, and like she said, you're the one training to be dropped off by the giant wind. As for me, I've got to figure out how to get more engineers to this planet."

Alistair sighed, then stood up. "You two have been a tremendous amount of help. I'm forever in your debt," he deadpanned. "I'll talk to ya later."

He and Obs left the apartment.

He wouldn't be able to think about her comment until the end of the day.

Later, when everything was finished and so many were dead, he'd wonder if the AllMother hadn't blundered. Was what he'd learned worth the destruction?

The AllMother went back to her bedroom after Alistair left.

She'd told him what she knew without her usual demeanor of taking nothing seriously, but she understood how grave the situation was quickly becoming. She was older than anyone to ever live—except her brother, obviously—so she rarely questioned her decisions.

She knew the end goal, and she mostly knew how to get there.

She also knew what she had to do: prepare *him*.

The AllMother went back to bed. She wouldn't be able to sleep anymore, but she figured she might as well try. Old people knew getting old was awful. The AllMother knew that times a thousand years. Not being able to sleep much was only one of the many discomforts her age brought.

I can't lay it down yet, though. Not until this is finished.

The AllMother's abilities weren't what they had once been, but it hadn't taken much of a gift to feel the massive armies that were coming for them. That much energy, that much bloodlust all directed at the man she'd waited her whole life to find? Her mind couldn't help but see them.

Only she knew she couldn't tell Alistair. The AllMother could die tomorrow, and what then? The man had to have confidence in his abilities. He had to know that he and he alone could finish this thing. He could not rely on anyone else to lead for him.

She hadn't even liked telling him what she had, to look at the sky. It was too damn obvious, but the gathering forces frightened her—so many, and not far away. The AllMother couldn't see them, but she felt them, and they gave off *evil*.

The AllMother understood that many people in this universe were killers. Alistair was a killer, as was she. There was a difference between the two of them and those traveling their way. The AllMother couldn't see those people clearly enough to know what they did, but she recognized sociopathy when she felt it.

A lot of people were coming for them because taking over this planet had created ripples Alistair hadn't thought through when he began.

The AllMother wasn't only worried about that, though. Another concern, and one that was growing, was her brother.

She hadn't heard from him in some time, nor did she feel his Myrmidons. He hadn't given up his chase; that was an impossibility, and that it appeared so indicated something was amiss.

The AllMother stared at the ceiling. Light would soon fall on the world, and she'd be forced to get back up again.

For now, though, she had one thought. *What are you doing, brother?*

The black-tentacled creatures that had been grown in a tank now traveled through the fifth dimension. The AllSeer had endowed them with the ability to move between dimensions, just as his ships could.

No human had ever seen anything like them. They were something new, a part of evolution outside of evolution. The most basic way to describe them would be to say they were both flesh and machine, but that wouldn't give the creational genius its due. Truthfully, that classification didn't work. They were something *new*.

Part of the AllSeer's genius was in creating horrors that could kill more efficiently than anything natural or manmade.

The tentacled things had played with each other in their tank, cutting the tentacles off one another and laughing about it, but they no longer did that. They were capable of something resembling thought, though it didn't have a linear pattern like that of humans or animals. At this moment, they were focused on one thing: finding the owner of the blood that had been spilled in their tank. Nothing else existed for them, and unlike creatures that could focus for a time, there would be nothing else until they found the owner.

It didn't matter how far away the individual was or whether he lived on the most densely populated planet the universe had ever known. They would find him, then they would kill him.

CHAPTER FIVE

The day was over, and Alistair was exhausted mentally and physically, though the things he'd done that day were nothing compared to some of his physical feats. He didn't know how many hours he'd worked, only that it was dark outside when he finally called it quits.

Obs was staring at him as he powered down the Data-Track. Alistair looked at the drathe. "You don't need me to go on a walk with you, you know. You're perfectly capable of doing it by yourself."

Obs barked at him, not in a friendly way.

"Fine." Alistair stood up. He'd been sitting for that majority of the day, and he figured it wouldn't hurt to get some kind of exercise, even if it was only walking outside with the drathe. "Let's go, but it's not going to be long. Don't get that in your head."

Animal and man went outside into the brisk night air. Alistair still hadn't gotten used to the colors of this strange planet. At night, something in the atmosphere lit strings of deep purple across the black sky, making it look as if the gods were trying to peek through.

Alistair had been rundown when he'd killed the men who controlled this place. He'd killed so many people and pushed so hard for so long that he'd felt less than human. Perhaps he'd even questioned if it was worth his soul to fight this war; he couldn't remember. His mind had been so frazzled, so frayed, that many of his thoughts were still gray now.

He felt better now. This respite here had let him recharge. He was ready to leave, though the feelings from conquering this place hadn't faded. He would never be the hero in a child's story. He understood that now. There was no pure confidence or lack of self-doubt in him. Perhaps heroes like that didn't exist, though sometimes the AllMother and the AllSeer seemed to be that kind.

Each was possessed by their goals. In some ways, Alistair thought they weren't very different from each other in that. They would both burn the entire universe to get what they wanted. For the AllMother, ending the Commonwealth justified her means.

The AllSeer's goals were less clear to any sane person, but he was the same.

Obs and Alastair were walking through the compound's grounds. The city was just outside the high walls, though the people who'd lived here had been in no danger. The creatures they bred would never rise up, and everyone else worked for the company.

Obs ran across the yard to the left of the brick trail they walked, rushing after one of the little vermin that lived in the trees. They looked like an Earth squirrel but with much larger, floppier ears and a curly tail, as well as being a neon green that matched the leaves they usually hid in almost perfectly.

Obs was the smartest animal Alistair had ever met, but even he liked to have his fun. Chasing those squirrel things provided that for him.

Alistair sighed, still exhausted despite this exercise. He'd done a lot of thinking about the AllMother and the AllSeer, but what of him?

Will you burn the universe to see me, Allie? his wife asked.

The truth?

He would. Still. He didn't *want* to, but if the universe forced him to burn it all, then that's what he'd do. Soul or no soul, he would see his wife again or die trying.

The small animal had made it up the tree, stopping halfway and turning around to taunt Obs. Most of the animals on this planet had been engineered after the originals were killed off by the colonizing humans. Alistair believed all the new ones had been endowed with a sense of humor.

He continued walking around the bend, knowing Obs would follow when he'd had enough fun teasing the squirrel creature. Alistair hadn't had time to consider what the AllMother had said, but he thought it might be the most important thing he'd heard today.

Look at the sky.

What was the old woman talking about?

He stopped and did as she'd told him, turning his head to the purple and black above. There were no clouds, just the planet's two moons across each other.

"What's up there?" he asked himself. "What do I need to learn that's so important?"

He rapidly thought through the possible answers.

There was only one that seemed to make any sense. Humans had been looking into the skies since they had eyes, and most of the time, they were looking for one thing: other lifeforms. If she was telling him to look at the sky now, it was because a giant wind was coming to get him.

There it was.

He'd either been too unfocused or too dumb to understand it then, but now it appeared obvious that someone was coming here. He didn't have to leave because the wind would come for him, and it was on the way.

The display showed Alistair outside her room, the drathe pacing at his side. The AllMother didn't have to see Alistair's face to know he'd figured out her little riddle from this morning; it was all over Obs. A ridge of hair stood up on his back, and he wouldn't stop walking back and forth as if patrolling for danger.

As far as Alistair's face, well, he looked less than pleased.

"Go ahead and open the door, Jeeves," she told the ever-present AI.

"Certainly, madam," Jeeves responded, and the door slid into the wall.

Alistair wasted no time, his broad shoulders nearly scraping the jambs as he stepped in. She knew he never thought about his size or the ruggedness of his physique. She also knew that when his enemies saw him, they would understand the man they dealt with was unlike anyone they'd seen before.

The AllMother was at her kitchen table with a cup of tea grown on this planet in front of her. Alistair rounded the corner, his presence sucking up the room's energy. He looked at the floor as he spoke, pacing as Thoreaux did. Obs, thank the gods, stopped patrolling and laid on the floor just outside the kitchen. He put his head between his paws and watched his master going to and fro.

"Would you like some tea, Alistair?" she asked.

He ignored her, reached the other end of the kitchen, and turned, still looking at the floor. "I'm going to leave the issue of why you didn't tell me to the side for the moment. Who is coming here? There's no other reason you would say to look at the sky, so who is it?"

The AllMother knew her role, and she also knew what Alistair wanted it to be. He wanted her to be his whipping post, but the AllMother understood that she was most likely his last teacher. None would come after. She wouldn't shrink from that role. "You were in my room about fourteen hours ago, Alistair. Not for long, though. You stood up and left. You didn't try to think about what I'd said. You just got mad that I wouldn't tell you exactly what you wanted to hear, and you left."

He stopped pacing and turned to her. It might have been the first time she'd seen something resembling rage in him. He'd gotten annoyed with her before, maybe even close to angry, but not like this. Her power would fall before him like autumn leaves in front of an oak. She could do nothing to stop this man if he wanted to hurt her.

"Who's coming?" he repeated in a low voice.

"I need you to answer my question first. Then we'll discuss yours."

He reached for the counter behind him and gripped the edge, his knuckles white. "Who is in charge here, you or me?"

"You."

"Then answer my question," he demanded.

The AllMother leaned back in her chair, put her hands on her knees, and stared at him for a few seconds. "You may be in charge of this movement, Alistair, but I think it's fair for you to remember that I built this from nothing. You know my story, and you know that to me, you're little more than a child. A newborn. Someone fresh from his mother's womb. Pluto wasn't the first world I saw burn. It wasn't even the second. I've witnessed empires grow and fall, surviving them all. I've been hunted since I was barely a woman by my brother, and I still live. Men and women have served at my feet for centuries, some perhaps greater than you, O Great Prometheus. They weren't *you*, but they understood what I'd seen and been through without knowing the full story. They listened to me, even if it wasn't what they wanted to hear. So, young man, decide now whether you respect me. Whether you trust me. If you don't, then certainly I'll answer your question. *Ave*, Prometheus."

He let go of the counter, and the rage left his face. His hands hung at his sides as his eyes gazed at the floor. After a second, he ambled to the table, pulled a chair out, and sat.

"I didn't think about it this morning because I was focused on other things. There's a world out there that I completely changed, and it's my responsibility to fix it and keep it from eating itself."

The AllMother didn't move. Her face didn't soften. She showed no change in emotion, but internally, if she could have wept with relief, she would have. The man could have walked out of the room, casting her to the side, and gone his own way. Instead, he was here and still willing to listen.

I chose well, she thought with more than a little thankfulness.

"Alistair, have you killed parents?" she asked.

"I suppose."

"Did you go to their house and care for their children? Did you make sure their offspring had food and shelter?"

He looked up, hurt on his face.

She raised a hand, her palm facing him. "No need to defend yourself. I understand. My point is, there were other times you didn't do *nearly* as much as you have here. You gave these gigantes a fighting chance to survive, and you've worked with the others to try to create an economy. It's commendable. It's more than any other warlord in this universe would do, I assure you. In doing so, though, you took your focus off your goal. Your mission. Even today, you went about your regular business instead of considering just about the only advice I've ever given you. That's why I didn't come out and tell you something was on the way here, Alistair—because you need to look out for those you lead. The more you take on, the greater your responsibilities and the more you have to look after. It was an honorable thing, coming here for these gigantes, but it was not our mission."

She paused. The former Titan was leaning his elbows on his knees and staring at the floor, taking his tongue-lashing without protest.

The AllMother softened her tone. "Do you know what the lesson is, Alistair? Do you understand what I was trying to teach you?"

He didn't answer for a few seconds. Obs stood up and padded over to lie beneath his chair and give him support.

"The obvious answer is if I'm leading the movement, then I need to lead toward our goal without sidetracking the entire thing."

She nodded. "That is the obvious answer. What's the non-obvious one?"

He didn't hesitate. He understood now. "That someone is always going to be coming after us. Even if the Commonwealth or the AllSeer isn't in front of us, *someone* will be trying to kill us."

"Exactly. For three months, we've been lucky. We've forgotten the threat to this rebellion. It's time we remembered."

"Okay." Alistair straightened and looked at her. "What is coming, or is that something else I have to figure out on my own?"

The AllMother finally smiled. "You know the answer to that. I've been spoon-feeding you from dawn to dusk. You need to figure out what's coming toward us."

He wasn't angry as he asked his next question. "You realize that every hour we wait, that's less time we have to prepare?"

"I do."

"It'll most likely cause more people to die. You understand that too?"

Her smile was gone as she nodded. "I understand. It will be worth it if it prepares you to get us back to Earth. You are the key that will unlock the door I've been staring at for a thousand years, and if this helps mold that key to fit the door, *anything* is worth it."

Alistair nodded, looking as if he'd thought about what she'd said. "I'll figure out who's coming then."

The hour was growing late. It was much later than Alistair thought he'd be up when he awoke this morning, but there was nothing to be done about it.

He'd walked with Obs outside for a bit, staring at the purple scars across the sky. He thought about how to figure this out. They could scan the sky and even the universe, but no technology to show the entirety of it existed. The universe was too vast and the ships traveling through it too small. Most likely, they weren't even in the third dimension but had jumped to the fourth, which would eliminate the ability to see them.

He finished his walk back at the compound. Obs was looking up at him. Alistair was able to read the drathe now, understanding what he wanted almost as well as Obs understood him. "You can go to bed," he told the animal. "I've got more to do yet."

The drathe reared up too quickly for Alistair to stop him and put his front paws on the man's chest. He gave his face two big licks, hit the ground again, and bounded off before Alistair had a chance to yell at him.

He shook his head, then wiped his face through the smile on it. Alistair had no idea how he'd gotten lucky enough to be soul-paired with an animal like Obs, but he was thankful for it.

There was only one person he wanted to talk to right now. Caesar was a gigante and part of a culture much richer and deeper than Alistair had ever imagined.

Caesar didn't stay with the rest of the council. He lived with the gigantes, and his reasoning had been sound.

"I can't teach them if they look at me as one of you. I am a gigante, and if I'm to free them, they have to know I'm the same as them."

Alistair could have taken a transport, but he decided to walk. He knew he wouldn't be sleeping tonight. He would think about this subject until it was solved because to do anything else would end with even more dead.

He headed to the outskirts of this singular city. The gigantes had never been allowed in, and as a whole, they didn't feel comfortable living inside the city limits. The "makers" were still a powerful remembrance, with some not believing them dead, only gone into hiding.

Caesar had his work cut out for him, that was for sure. Alistair had seen little of him since they'd taken ownership of the planet.

It was a three-mile walk to where Caesar stayed, and Alistair traveled fairly quickly. He didn't know if the gigante was up or how much help he'd be, but he wanted to see his friend. They hadn't known each other for long, but that didn't matter when they'd been through as much as they had.

He reached the tent-town they lived in. They were only a few miles from state-of-the-art buildings, yet they preferred the housing they'd had as children, large tents that could hold ten or more gigantes at a time. Fires blazed within their small city.

Alistair walked past tents and fires. The gigantes knew, feared, and respected him. It showed how good a job Caesar was doing that they didn't bow to him, but he could see the awe on their faces as he headed toward where Caesar slept, the firelight not allowing their emotions to hide.

He arrived at the tent. It was sized for a single gigante to sleep in since that was the way their clan leaders were usually housed, the only luxury given to them. Caesar had taken it, but not out of any need for luxury. It simply allowed for privacy when he spoke one-on-one with others.

Alistair raised the tent's flap and peered inside. Caesar was on the other side, seated with his legs folded beneath him. A large sheet of paper was before him, with lines and words crisscrossing it. The words were written in the gigantes' language, so Alistair couldn't have read it if he'd wanted to.

Caesar looked up. "*Ave*, Prometheus."

Alistair smiled at the greeting. "You mind if I come in for a minute?"

The giant shook his massive head. "I've missed you, Pro. It is good to see you." The gigantes spoke a stilted form of the language, sometimes overly formal, sometimes missing words. Alistair found it endearing for some reason.

"It's good to see you too." He stepped inside the tent, a massive thing that allowed him to stand up fully. There was no pole in the middle, but the gigantes used metal up the sides and at the base, which kept the thing sturdy against the elements as well as gravity. Alistair took a seat a meter or so away from the giant. "How are things going?"

Frustration dawned on his face. "What is the saying? Herding cats? That's what this is like. Some understand, and some are swearing their life to you. It is a difficult thing, changing the way someone thinks."

Alistair chuckled. "Now you see what I had to deal with when you joined."

He shook his head. "I was never this bad, Pro. Not possible."

Alistair's smile widened. He knew just how bad the giant had been when it came to understanding he wasn't someone's slave.

The giant shook his head again, then found Alistair's eyes. "What brings you to the gigantes, Pro? Are things okay?"

"Yes and no. Governing the planet is going okay, but something else has come up."

"That is the way of things, I think," Caesar said. "Something always comes up. I often think back to before I met you. Life wasn't necessarily easier, but it was simpler. I went where I was told, killed who I was told to kill. Now?" He rolled his eyes, and it made Alistair laugh aloud. "Now I have five hundred things going on at once."

Alistair liked hearing the gigante talk like this. He was

expanding as a being, becoming much more than the simple killer he'd once been. "How's Nero?"

"He comes and goes as he wants, which is to be expected," Caesar said. "He was here this morning and said he thought you might stop by."

Alistair raised an eyebrow. "Did he really?" Nero was a very different gigante, one they called "touched." From what he could tell, he had something similar to Alistair's sight, the ability to see things that hadn't happened yet. He seemed to be able to control the damned thing, which Alistair couldn't do.

Caesar nodded. "He's usually right about those things, so I've been expecting you. Now, enough catch-up. Why are you here, Pro?"

Alistair slowly laid down and stared up at the tent. The top of it was transparent, allowing whoever lay inside to see the sky. The purple lights stretched across his vision. He rehashed what had happened today and what he was supposed to do: figure out who was coming for them.

When he finished, he lay silently staring up.

"That seems simple, Pro," the giant told him.

Alistair's eyes widened. "Yeah? Simple? What do you recommend then, Caesar?"

The giant shrugged. "Use your mind. Your mind has shown you the future, saved my life, and any number of other things. There's no reason it can't do this. That's what I would do."

Alistair opened his mouth to say something, but he couldn't find any words. His eyes were wide because what the gigante had said sounded so simple, but he didn't understand how impossibly hard—

His wife's voice interrupted his thoughts. *It's impossibly hard, Allie, because you're making it so. There's no reason you can't do this, except in your mind, you've gotten to the place where you think you don't understand yourself.* You're *making this impossible. No one else.*

She wasn't usually wrong.

The giant certainly wasn't wrong because what was he supposed to use if not his mind? The technology didn't exist to do what was necessary. The AllMother had known, and the only way that could have happened was her abilities.

That was what she wanted of him. That was the next lesson: to figure out how to use his mind.

Alistair closed his eyes without saying anything more. Caesar remained quiet as well, though Alistair no longer focused on the giant.

He knew this place much better than he had months ago. He was in a place his mind had somehow created. It was of this universe and at the same time not. It wasn't necessary for him to come here every time, but with something this massive, he needed to begin here.

Alistair felt a rush as his black place pushed through the clouds. His body was below in Caesar's tent, but *this* part of him was now above the clouds and approaching the limits of the planet's atmosphere. Soon, it would be in space.

He had never attempted anything like this, but he found he could do it easily. The black space behind his eyes was now populated with red dots he knew were stars, colored differently in this strange place. Space stretched for as far as he could see, and he knew he could rush forward again if he wanted to. Perhaps even visit other planets.

That wouldn't get him what he needed, though.

You can do this, Luna told him. *What do you need to find?*

Those who wish me harm, was the cold answer, and Alistair understood he had to step away. His thoughts, his questions, were not what he needed now. He needed the warrior part of himself. He needed Prometheus.

The warrior stepped forward. In the tent, there was no change in the man's body. His eyes remained closed. His breathing remained slow and steady.

In the black space of his mind where he stared at red stars, Prometheus understood what needed to be done. He pushed his mind higher, breaking through the outer limits of the planet's atmosphere and thrusting himself into space. The red stars slowly spun as he turned, getting a 360-degree view of the area around him.

He saw only stars.

That made sense. He wouldn't see anything here in this third dimension. They were traveling in the fourth, so that was where he had to go if he wished to see them.

Prometheus shoved...not up but *in*. He pierced the thin membrane that separated the two dimensions. He had no idea if any human had ever done that before, but he didn't care. The warrior had only one purpose at that moment— to find those who wished him harm.

In the fourth dimension, the red stars disappeared. There was only blackness until he turned a hundred and eighty degrees. Then he saw them.

They appeared as a massive red cloud with small deep-red dots inside it. The cloud was rushing toward him with unfathomable speed, and it spread almost all the way across Pro's vision. It was a force unlike anything he'd ever encountered, and it was coming at his planet faster than he thought possible.

Prometheus now understood that time was short. These violent creatures would be here soon, and he had to prepare their defenses, yet he wanted to see what was coming. He wanted to lay eyes on those he would soon kill.

He thrust his mind out, covering untold kilometers at untold rates. The cloud before him grew larger until he could see nothing else, then he was inside it.

It was no longer a cloud but ships of all sizes—dreadnoughts and corvettes, more than Pro had seen within the Commonwealth. He turned slowly, examining the armada, amazed. He could hardly believe anyone would send such a force for him, yet here it was, and he was inside it.

Prometheus would leave the questions for Alistair. He wanted to see who had coalesced this armada.

Three ships shone brighter red than the others, one on either end of the force and one in the middle. Prometheus' mind went forth, hitting the ones on either side first. He found the men in charge, one fat with a scar down his face, one muscular but more effeminate. In a one-on-one battle, Prometheus had no fear of either of the men, even though their eyes gave them away as killers. This wasn't a one-on-one battle, though.

In the middle ship, he found a woman.

The other two were important. They each controlled a third of this giant force. Prometheus knew now, though, where the danger lay—this woman. She was thin, not quite emaciated, but only a week's worth of meals from it. Her hair was an ice-like blonde, and her eyes were the palest blue he'd ever seen. She sat in a chair with one leg crossed over the other, her face showing no emotion as she stared at the panels in front of her.

This woman would see the end of his insurrection if she could.

This woman would kill him, and she had summoned the greatest army he'd ever seen to do it.

CHAPTER SIX

"This isn't good," Ares said as he stared at the monitors. "You know that, right? This wasn't what I planned when we started."

Veena ignored him from the captain's chair. She was hammering on a digital keyboard and yelling commands to the ship's AI, none of which were having any effect on their ability to navigate.

Ares didn't understand the details of what was happening, but he didn't need to. He understood the larger picture, which was that their ship's velocity had been decreased by half at first, then another half, and now they were starting to reverse course.

None of which was due to Veena's commands.

Ares was on the bridge—if it could be called that, given the ship's small size—wearing civilian clothes. There was only one thing he needed to know right now. "Do I need to suit up?"

He was referring to his MechSuit since if a battle was coming, he wasn't going into it with just his Whip. The panels in front of him showed there was nothing around them, just the darkness of space and stars burning in the distance.

Veena ignored his question and shouted at the AI, "What is causing this? Eliminate all functions that aren't mandatory to sustain life on the ship and focus all remaining compute power on what is causing this."

"Please hold," the AI said from the speakers above them.

An eerie silence fell on the bridge. Veena quit pounding on the keyboard. There seemed to be no sense in it because nothing they had done had stopped the reversal. They had to be in a tractor beam and the ship doing it had to be powerful, which made a StealthBlanket almost impossible.

Ares honestly didn't know how this was happening, and neither did Veena.

Two *long* minutes passed in that silence, with Ares trying to decide whether he should run to his quarters and put the MechSuit on or wait to hear what was happening. He was just about to leave the bridge when the AI came back on.

"It's a planet," the AI said.

Veena stood. "Show me."

The images on the monitors rotated, though the only way Ares could tell was from the movement of stars in the background. There wasn't another reference point visible.

When the monitors finally stopped, the area looked the same.

"What am I looking at?" Veena demanded.

"A planet that isn't on any known maps. It has no moons or stars and appears to reflect space. It is invisible to the eye and to all scans I was able to do until the last one, which showed a rectangular shape."

Ares spoke up. "Planets aren't rectangular."

"It depends on your definition of a planet. This one appears to be manmade, though if so, it is the largest known manmade creation. Or not known, as the case may be."

Ares looked at Veena, but she was still staring at the monitor. "Can you highlight the rectangle for me? What does a thermal scan show?"

A long green box appeared in the middle of the screen. Ares did some quick math from the scaling and saw that it was about half the size of Earth length-wise and a quarter width-wise. It was a massive structure.

"There is no heat escaping from the planet," the AI said. "That is one of the reasons I was unable to detect it at first. The outside is the temperature of space."

"That's impossible," Veena whispered. "Life can't exist without heat, and there's no way something that size could stop any heat leakage across the entire perimeter."

"No heat can be detected," the AI repeated.

Ares asked the only question that he thought mattered. "How long until we're at the structure?"

"With no changes in speed or trajectory, five standard hours. If a speed increase is projected, along with a concurrent projected decrease before contact, one standard hour."

"I'm suiting up," Ares told Veena. "You two try to figure out what is inside that box."

Ares, son of Adrian, left the bridge to prepare for war.

Veena remained seated and stared at the highlighted box on the monitor. She was trying to figure out what could have created it, as well as when. How long had it been out here in space with nothing around it for billions of kilometers?

Veena had been at the ship's whim since they left the refueling station. They'd repeated the digits to the AI, and that had been all they could do. For the past forty-eight hours, the ship had traveled in the fourth dimension, dropping down into the third only moments before.

"Gods," she whispered, having missed the obvious connection. Whatever map existed in those digits had brought them to this black waystation in the middle of nowhere. It was not accidental that they were being pulled into the black box. It had been inevitable from the moment they had given the coordinates to their ship.

Veena flicked a few of the controls to see if she could marshal any of the ship's weapons.

"The planet also has control of our weapons and biological systems," the AI said.

"Biological systems?" Veena could hardly believe that. The tractor could theoretically be so powerful that the ship's turrets, plasma, and other guns couldn't fire. To take control of the biological systems, though?

"Yes, I've confirmed three times," the AI responded.

"Have they changed anything?" Veena asked, frantic for the first time.

"Not yet. I'm continuously monitoring and will alert you if anything is altered."

"Try to make contact with it," Veena said. "See if there's any willingness to communicate."

"I have been, and so far, none of my attempts have gained a response."

This AI was a good one, and that was about the only positive thing Veena could say since her idiotic decision to leave the Commonwealth's graces. In her career, she'd rarely relied on an AI, trusting her instincts and decision-making abilities. Right now, though, she was glad she had this one. "Is there anything I'm not thinking of? Anything that might make a difference?"

The AI answered quickly. "Everything that can be done has been done. As I'm sure you've already considered, this was planned long before we arrived."

This was planned long before we arrived...

Veena stood then, understanding that she wouldn't be able to do anything from the chair. She couldn't pilot her way out of this.

She jogged to Ares' quarters, wondering if he'd already figured out what she'd just been told.

He was in his full MechSuit, his helmet retracted into the neckline so his head remained visible. He looked at her through the open doorway with raised eyebrows. "Anything new?"

"Whatever that thing is," she said as she took a step closer, "it's been waiting for us. We might not even be the first people to come through here. If not, I imagine it was waiting for them too."

She saw that he hadn't been thinking about it, but it only took a few moments for him to understand her meaning. Young, sometimes arrogant, but not stupid.

He nodded, then reached for the Whip that lay on the cot next to him. "I don't know whether that's a good or bad thing. If others have been here and that piece of paper still existed back where we found it, I'm leaning toward it being bad."

"I agree. It might also explain why the pirates we stole it from didn't rush to get here. Maybe they knew more than we do."

Ares hooked the Whip onto his suit. "You need to suit up, too. This might be the end of our non-lengthy lives, but I'm going to do everything I can not to let that be so."

Veena looked at him for a second and realized that for perhaps the first time, her life was in his hands. Before there'd always been someone like Hel, or they'd been in her domain: space flight. She'd never been at his mercy like she would be now since they were entering his domain—hand-to-hand combat. Killing where you could see the enemy's eyes.

Please be as good as you think you are, she said to herself. Aloud, she told him, "I'll be back in twenty minutes. That should give us ten before we make contact."

Ares was solemn as he nodded and bent to take a knee. Veena remained standing in the doorway and watched as his hand and forearm armor retracted. She knew what he was about to do, the ritual all Titans did before battle. He was no longer a Titan, but he continued to say the words. Continued cutting his arm. Continued wiping the blood on his face.

For some reason Veena couldn't place, she took comfort in that. She didn't watch as he repeated the words of old but went to prepare herself for what came next. It was enough to know he was saying them.

"The planet is attempting to shut me—"

The AI fell silent. Ares glanced at the speakers, realizing the planet had attempted nothing. It had succeeded in shutting the AI down.

He and Veena were in the ship's cargo bay, and the whole room suddenly shook. Ares' head snapped to the bay's door, figuring danger would come from there first. The shaking was the ship docking with the structure.

"They waited until we didn't need the AI anymore before shutting it down," Veena whispered from his side.

"Or until we would think we didn't need it. Truthfully, I don't think it's done us much good since we got inside this thing's pull. They just didn't want us to panic."

Veena stood next to him in armor. It wasn't anything like the MechSuit he wore, but they had managed to find different pieces in their travels. She had a MechPulse strapped across her back and a beam in her right hand. He'd told her to use the beam until it overheated, then the pulse. It was a heavy weapon, and he thought her muscles might tire too quickly if she went in with that first.

A few minutes passed with nothing happening, just the two of them standing in silence, their ship either connected to this foreign structure or sitting inside it. Neither of them knew which.

The lights in the cargo bay shut off and Ares' helmet auto-switched to dark view, though Veena would be able to see very little. "Get close to me," he told her.

She stepped slightly behind his left foot, close enough

that her body was touching his suit. "Don't get any ideas," she whispered.

Ares appreciated the attempt at levity. "You're not my type," he responded, his helmet making it sound like a robot was speaking.

The bay door began opening. Ares' heads-up display was feeding him all the information it could. "Stay here," he told Veena and took ten steps forward before stopping. He wanted the suit to analyze the atmosphere of the place, though they didn't have a great plan if it was poisonous. Mainly, Veena would run deep into the ship and try to seal off a room from airflow. Given that this structure had nearly complete control over their ship, the safest option was for the atmosphere to be copacetic.

The suit quickly diagnosed the air coming in, and the HUD displayed **Atmosphere 99.97% similar to Earth. No danger.**

"Air is safe," he called back.

The bay door finished opening, and Ares found himself staring into a lightless room. They appeared to be inside the structure rather than docked to the outside. His HUD told him the temperature of the platform they rested on was nearly identical to the temperature inside the ship. "Temp is fine," he said as Veena approached him. "Something in here is generating heat, and they have the means to keep it from escaping."

Veena was quiet as she stood slightly behind him and to the left. Ares went forward but saw nothing and no one on the platform. He stepped off the bay ramp onto a solid surface. The area was as dark as the cargo bay had been, if not darker. "Can you see anything?"

"My eyes are adjusting some, but no, not really. My right hand is on your left elbow, so don't go too quickly, or you'll leave me behind."

"Got it," Ares responded. For all their bitching and the early distrust and the arguments, at that moment, they only had each other. Perhaps that had been true since they had both abandoned their posts with the Commonwealth, but neither had felt it as clearly as when they stepped onto an alien structure, alone except for each other.

Ares' duty, which had been to the Commonwealth, was now to the woman at his side.

There was no welcoming party, no group of soldiers to kill them. There was nothing but this black room and a hall leading off to the left. "We're going forward," he said. "There's a hallway to the left, and unless you have a better idea, I vote we follow it."

"There's no moving that ship without doing something here first, so yeah, that's got my vote too. Let's go."

Ares gave a nod that no one could see and then started forward. They walked slowly, Ares' HUD telling him when Veena's hand lost touch with his suit. It also mapped out where the hallway was taking them, keeping up with the turns and elevations. They appeared to be winding around the edge of the structure, but there were no other hallways connected to this one. Ares couldn't go left or right because there was no left or right, just this hallway leading them to what appeared to be nowhere.

"How long have we been in here?" he asked the HUD.

Two standard hours, it displayed.

Ares stopped walking.

"What is it?" Veena said.

"We've been winding around the tunnel for two hours so far. Cast forward," he told the HUD.

Blue light shot onto the floor in front of his feet, allowing Veena to see the trail they'd taken. She shielded her eyes for a second while they adjusted to the new light.

After a few moments, she knelt and slowly traced her hand over the blue trail. "You see what it is?"

"No."

She traced the trail again, this time from their current spot back to the ship. This time, Ares saw it. "That's the first digit from the paper."

"Exactly." She stood up and kept staring at the blue line. "Wherever this hallway leads, it's going to resemble the second digit, then the third, and so on. The question is, why?"

Ares didn't have an answer.

"Also, and maybe even more importantly, have you had the ability to cast a light like that the entire time?"

Ares raised both eyebrows, feeling embarrassed and moronic. He hadn't even thought about it. "Yeah, I suppose I have."

Veena looked like she wanted to slap him. "Perhaps it's a good idea to start using it. Might make this a bit quicker, yes?"

Ares ignored the comment and switched from the tiny blue light on the floor to a wider floodlight that revealed the hallway to them.

"WHY ARE YOU HERE?"

The words boomed from the walls, floor, and ceiling. They came from everywhere at once, loud in a way human voices couldn't be.

Ares turned to Veena. Her eyes were wide, her mouth slightly open. Both hands were on her beam, pointing it at the floor. She nodded slightly, and Ares followed her gaze.

A droid stood a few meters away, with no evidence of where it had come from. It remained as still as a cadaver, nothing on it moving, nothing showing any sign of life.

"*WHY ARE YOU HERE?*" Again the voice roared from the structure, causing the MechSuit to turn down the volume in Ares' helmet.

Ares' unholstered his Whip, letting the three lasers unfurl almost to the floor. The deep-red crimson that had been so feared on Earth was unknown in this strange part of the galaxy. The droid at the end of the hall probably knew as much about his callsign and his weapon as it did his father's lessons when Ares was a boy. Nothing. To the droid and whoever else controlled his ship, he was an unwanted intruder. More, those in control here apparently felt that anything within range of their tractor beam was an intruder, whether or not it entered this strange floating structure.

"We're here because you forced us to be. Kindly let us get back on our ship, and we'll be here no more," he answered. For all he knew, the makers of this place might think him a droid too, given his armor and the voice emanating from his helmet.

"*YOU'RE NOT WORTHY,*" the voice roared from the walls.

The droid came to life. A strip about an inch wide and five inches long that ran across its head turned a bright neon-blue. The droid's arms ended without hands or other appendages, but now neon-blue lasers shot out of both of them. Holes opened across its thin, metal body, and shorter blue lasers created a defensive shield around its torso and legs. Ares understood that if he got too close, those things would burn through his suit.

He turned his head to the left. "Veena, don't shoot, no matter what. The area is too close, and I don't know if these walls are reflective. You could send a laser bouncing twenty times in here. I'll handle this."

"Handle it fast then, Titan."

Ares looked up.

The droid was rushing toward him, its neon-blue laser arms pumping hard. The sounds of its metal feet colliding with the floor echoed off the walls.

Ares didn't hesitate. He lashed his Whip forward, all three lasers slicing through the air and meeting no resistance as he cut through the droid.

It collapsed to the floor with three large incisions cut through its head and both shoulders. Smoke rose into the air around both of them.

"What in the gods' names was that about?" he whispered. That had been too easy. It had been beyond easy. A half-trained boy could have killed that thing.

He caught his breath at what came next. He'd never seen anything like it. The holes he'd cut into the droid began closing. The metal that had split turned liquid to repair the gashes, then hardened again. This continued until the metal husk looked as if it had never been harmed.

"Get back, Veena," Ares said.

The walls asked their question once more. "WHY ARE YOU HERE?"

The droid rose off the floor as if the artificial gravity

had no effect on it. It didn't use its arms or legs to stand, just *lifted* until it was upright again, the blue strip on its head alive and lasers shooting out the ends of its arms.

It came at Ares. He lashed with his Whip in the same fashion, this time wanting to understand rather than harm the droid.

Its two arms blocked the Whip, crossing its lasers over one another. At the same time, it kicked out. Ares' Whip was wrapped around the lasers, so he turned his body sideways, dodging the kick. He used a simple twist to move to the opposite side of the droid's body, unfurled his Whip at the same time, and brought it down on the creature's unprotected skull.

It dropped to the floor as it had before.

Ares looked over the momentarily deactivated droid and found Veena. "It's learning. It's going to keep adapting to me and the way I fight."

"Can you kill it?"

The metal was liquifying and repairing itself as they spoke.

"Not yet," Ares said. His Whip formed a straight spear, and he shoved it through the thing's chest. The liquifying metal stopped flowing. He left the spear continuing to burn inside the droid. "Well, that's working, but I'm not going to leave my Whip here."

Veena's beam was pointed at the droid, though her finger was off the trigger. "You might have to."

"WHY ARE YOU HERE?"

"I'm seriously tired of that question," Ares said as he heard a new sound.

"Liquid metal" were the two words that came to his

mind. He turned toward where the sound came from and froze.

The walls *rippled*, a wave running across them from the far end to where he stood. He watched as they fell into one another, though that wasn't the correct way to describe what happened. It was all his mind could come up with, though. The result was a circular area instead of the hall he'd been standing in, and three other droids now stood where walls had been moments before.

"The droids are part of the ship," Veena said. "It's part of them."

Ares didn't give a damn about what they were part of. He understood what they were capable of, and that was all that mattered. He assessed the situation as quickly and coldly as he could. Worst-case scenario, these droids and this structure were a hive mind. What one droid learned, the others would as well. They would continue adapting to him until he could no longer fight back. Then they would kill him.

Ares amplified his hearing, needing to know when something in the structure was changing. The sound of liquid metal flowing would tell him.

Lasers shot from the other three droids' arms, each droid using a different color—yellow, green, and purple. Ares reached behind him and pulled his Whip out of the droid's body, knowing that doing so would allow it to heal.

"You want me to shoot them? I should have enough room," Veena said from a couple of meters back.

"Not until there's no other choice. I have some room yet. They don't know much about what I'm capable of, so maybe I can find a way to kill them."

"Do it, then."

He didn't know how quickly these things learned or if they could extrapolate what they did know to future acts. He was about to find out.

Ares took two running steps and leaped, then thrust the Whip at Purple, sending the laser through the top of the droid's metal skull. It had tried to block him from the first attack he'd done, the simple lash, but his Whip had come from somewhere else.

So they learn slowly, he thought. *Good.*

He moved across the circular area like an evil dancer, graceful but carrying death everywhere he went. His Whip carved and cut, slicing down droids as they came for him. He went through all three of the new ones just as Blue was rising.

It mimicked his leaping strike. He stepped to the side and cut the thing in half.

That would have to kill it.

The others were already rising. Ares turned, his Whip at his side. The three came at him, each doing a perfect copy of one of the moves he'd already used. He understood the forms as well as any man to ever live and knew how to counter each. He made quick work of the three, then brought his attention back to the one he'd cut in half.

The godsdamn thing was pulling itself toward the other half. The liquid metal was stretching out, grabbing the floor, and tugging like a million tiny arms. Wires and metal frayed as the outer shell continued its work of reattaching itself.

"Try the head!" Veena shouted. Her beam was raised, though her finger still wasn't on the trigger.

Ares stepped over the lower half to the upper and brought his Whip across the thing's neck. He kicked the head, his metal boot clanging into the skull, and it flew across the newly-created room.

The other three were back up, and Ares now understood the truth. It wasn't just the learning that would kill him. These things did not tire. They could die a thousand deaths and come back fresh each time. He, on the other hand? How long could he continue this? Even though he was in peak physical condition, he would eventually falter.

"Stand over that head and shoot at it every time it tries to heal!" he shouted at Veena.

Then he went to work. It was monotonous, the continual cutting and rising. Three, four, five times, he killed the droids. Each time they rose from the dead. Blue remained unable to heal as long as Veena kept firing at its skull, but even that wouldn't work forever.

The minutes passed, and he came up with no other ideas. The only addition was kicking another skull over to Veena, who continued firing. She switched her beam with her pulse, but soon they realized even that wouldn't work.

Ares trotted backward as the two he'd freshly killed lay on the other side of the room. He glanced at the metal skulls.

"They're healing faster," Veena told him. She fired the pulse at the one on the left.

"Yeah, mine are too." Ares was winded, and it seemed the faster he killed them, the faster they shot back up. The two were already on their feet and coming at him.

He moved slowly away from Veena, waiting for them to make a move. They had started coordinating their attacks, using his forms against him in ways that complimented each other. They weren't advanced yet, but it wouldn't be long.

He blocked the attack on the right with his Whip and saw his first mistake. He ducked, ready to kick with his suit, but the droid wasn't where it should have been.

It was behind him.

He slammed his left hand on the ground, thrust himself up, and twirled horizontally in the air.

The droid's laser sliced, cutting deep into his suit.

Ares landed two meters away, the HUD displaying the damage. It hadn't hit his body, but his reaction time had kept it at bay by only centimeters.

On one knee, he looked at Veena. Her eyes were wide. Smoke trailed up to the ceiling from where his suit had burned.

For the first time since this ludicrous battle started, he was down while the two droids remained standing.

Ares closed his eyes for a moment and saw his father's face. There were no words, no lessons, just the hard look of a man who had loved him and raised him as well as he could.

Ares had brought them here. He had been the one who wanted this algorithm. He realized he would die here, and there wasn't anything he could do about it. These machines would continue coming, wearing him down battle by battle, until he lay on his back and their lasers devoured him.

He opened his eyes. The two robots stood in front of him, their arm lasers pointing toward the floor. "Veena, I'm going to hold them off as long as I can. I've got time yet, but not forever. I want you to run. Try to board the ship and get it to take off. Do whatever you can. I'm not going to live past this, and if you stay, you won't either."

Ares' Whip had shortened. He held it in his right hand, still on a knee. Veena's MechPulse pointed at the skulls on the ground, and even from where he knelt, he saw how quickly they were repairing themselves. Their time here was nearly at an end. "There's nothing else you can do," he told her. "Save yourself. I'm sorry I brought us here."

Veena gave a single nod, and in it, Ares saw self-hate, anger, and the realization that this structure would end them both. Even if she tried to escape, her chance of success was small.

He nodded back and Veena was gone, disappearing down the hall that had brought them here.

Ares rose to his feet. The faceplate on his helmet pulled back, showing the blood beneath his eyes. It was smeared from sweat and made it look like he'd been weeping blood.

"See it and die."

———

Veena ran for five minutes before she stopped. She knew they had walked for two hours to get here, but what did that mean? In a structure like this, where droids were made from the walls, she could run forever.

She stood in the middle of the hallway and turned, facing where she'd come from. Where Ares still was.

"What's it matter?" she whispered to herself. "If I live, if I leave him behind? What's it matter where these halls lead, even if it's to the greatest ship I've ever seen? If I leave him back there, every hallway will only lead to one place as long as I breathe. Back here."

Veena had risen to Primus, and given the chance, she'd left another Primus to fight a battle for her. It was the coward's way out, and even five minutes of living as a coward were far too much for her.

She strapped the MechPulse to her back, and with the StarBeam holstered, ran as fast as she could back to the man she'd left.

———

Ares didn't know how long he fought. Time no longer mattered, only the ability to remain standing. To remain cutting. To remain *fighting*.

He thought back to the fight against the much-less-talented boy. The one who'd kept coming, who'd inflicted wounds methodically and never used flash to win. Ares had no idea what had happened to that kid or if he was still alive, a good husband to someone. Maybe he was raising kids, an all-around Commonwealth gold-star citizen.

What happened to him didn't matter either, but the fundamentals he'd used that day did.

Ares went back to the fundamentals. Everything he used was learned, adapted, and put into an ever-increasing knowledge bank of skills—all of which would be used to kill him.

Still, he fought. There were flashes of brilliance, of speed, of strength, but his body was wearing down. He killed the droids, and they were reborn. His MechSuit collected scars as their laser arms got past his slowing defenses.

Eventually, he found his back against the wall. The four stood in front of him. His heart was beating rapidly, breath heaving in and out of his lungs. The droids showed no fatigue. No scars. No sign that they had been beaten even once.

This is it, he thought.

"Father," he whispered, "I have not forgotten you or what you taught me. I hope my life and my death have made you proud."

He brought his Whip up in front of him, the laser's strands twirling around each other to form a sword-like weapon. He grabbed the hilt with both hands.

"Duck."

He and the droids looked at the circular room's entrance. Veena was back, a MechPulse in her hands.

Ares didn't have time to question or refuse. He simply ducked and rolled to his left.

She fired the weapon, and the droids were slammed into the wall before slumping to the floor, dead yet again.

Ares lurched to his feet. "What the fuck are you doing?"

Veena walked closer to him, the MechPulse aimed at the self-repairing droids. "It seems every bad decision I've ever made has been when I was around you. I don't see any reason to stop that now."

Ares heard her words and understood the truth beneath them. She wouldn't lose her honor to man or machine, or whatever the fuck this creation in the middle of nowhere was.

He said nothing, only raised his weapon, again ready to die—this time with a friend at his side.

The droids all rose off the floor as if they were puppets on strings.

When the walls spoke, gone was the thunder of gods. It was replaced by a voice that sounded human. A male voice. "That's enough."

The droids' lasers retracted into their arms. The laser spikes on their torsos and legs disappeared back inside. The strips across their skulls dimmed and then went out.

Neither Ares nor Veena lowered their weapons. It wasn't until Ares heard the sound of the liquid metal to his right that he looked over. Another hallway had appeared, the wave running away from them this time, down into the darkness.

"Come," the voice said. "You will have safe passage."

A single line of lights lit up on both sides of the new hall, allowing them to see where they were walking. Ares looked back at the droids, but they were gone.

Veena was still staring at where they'd been. "The wall, it came out and got them."

Ares was exhausted, though that word only hinted at what his body felt like.

"Come," the voice said again.

Ares could think of nothing else to do but listen to the voice. His mind was non-functional, and thank the gods Veena understood.

"Let's go." She took the lead, and they walked down the new passage. It took just minutes this time, though Ares didn't bother looking at his HUD. He followed Veena and prayed they didn't have to fight again. He would defend them if necessary but understood the result would come fast and wouldn't be in their favor.

The hall sloped downward, which meant they were walking into the middle of the structure. It ended in a globe-like room with only the floor not curved.

A man sat on a ledge that came up to Ares' head. His feet hung off it, and the clothes he wore were very strange. Ares thought he might be able to place them if he wasn't so drained, but for the moment, they were lost to him.

"Romulus de Livius and Veena de Ragnimus." The man's voice crackled as he spoke, which was the first hint that they weren't looking at a living human. "Do you know who I am?"

Both of the Earthborn shook their heads.

"No one who has made it this far has known, so don't feel bad." His feet dangled over the ledge, lazily kicking. "Since you're here, I assume you're after the algorithm. This place has been here for many centuries, and no one has come here except for that reason. It's true for you also?"

"It is," Veena answered.

Ares was half-paying attention to the man and half-reading his HUD, trying to understand this room. The man was a holovid, reasonably well kept up given the distance of this place from neighboring habitable planets. Ares assumed the droids did the upkeep. There was also some kind of AI at work here.

"Unfortunately for you two, I am not the algorithm. Your journey, if you continue onward, merely passes through this place."

"What is this place?" Veena asked.

"There's a long version and a short version. Which would you prefer to hear?"

Ares spoke up. "The short version."

"Good enough for me. If you get to the algorithm, you will probably hear the long version anyway." The holovid interlaced his fingers, turned his hands palm out, and stretched his knuckles. "At some point in the distant past, a group of people found the same key you did, typed it into a ship-based AI, and went after the algorithm. As you've no doubt deduced by now, the original ship that contained the algorithm survived, or there would most likely be a plethora of the algorithms in existence."

Ares glanced at Veena. She refused to look his way.

"Nearly every group that went after the algorithm died. One, however, did not, and they built this place. They are my creators. I do not know who they are, whether they are human or another species. I do not know anything about them except that they seemed to know a bit about me. What you're looking at is a representation of the man who set the algorithm loose. Whether I resemble him or not, who can say? I'm rambling now. Let me get back on topic. The group that created this place took many, many years to do so, and when they were finished, they left it forever."

"Why?"

"Why is the universe expanding at an ever-increasing rate? Who can say? If I had to guess, it's because whatever awaited them at the algorithm was much too deadly to defeat. I *think* this is a testing ground for what comes next, but I was not endowed with that knowledge either."

Veena shook her head, obviously not buying the story. "A group or species advanced enough to create this place wouldn't fear anything. If you can create a self-contained ecosystem that continuously repairs itself, you can find that algorithm."

The holovid shrugged. "Perhaps you're right. Or perhaps there's more to the story than either of us knows. I don't have the answer, and neither of you two does either. I only know when you have passed the test, which you did."

A question came to Ares. "Since you were built, how many people or groups have come through here?"

"You are the tenth."

Ares asked, "How many passed the test?"

"You were the second."

"And the others? What happened to them?"

The holovid replied, "I am fairly certain they failed. They would have most likely had to come back this way, and there has been no sight of them."

"What happens next?" Veena asked.

"That's up to you. Both of you understand the risks involved now and that the likelihood of success is near zero. I have given your ship back its full power, plus given your AI some helpful tips for the future, regardless of whether you go on or go back. If you go forward, the digits you put in will take over, and you'll go to the next spot on the trip. If you go home," he said, shrugging, "you go home."

Veena finally looked at Ares. He had retracted his helmet into his neckline so they could see each other.

"I don't have a home," she said.

"Yeah, I don't think I do either."

"You believe it's real?"

Ares was quiet for a moment. When he answered, it was

truthful. "I don't know. Something is at the end of this, though, and after what just happened, I'd like to find out what."

Veena looked at the floor with a smile on her face. "Every bad decision, they're all made around you. Fuck it. Let's go see what killed all the people before us."

CHAPTER SEVEN

Hector de Gracilis, the grandson of Caius de Gracilis, had just made his first trip to Earth. It was a short trip, and the fourth-dimensional travel caused no distress to his body.

The landing had been simple, and he understood his grandfather's wishes. He was not to be seen until the meeting with the Propraetors. Even the servants of the Gracilis lineage would not have access to Hector.

Which was fine with the young man. In some ways— many ways—he was naive. He knew nothing about politics. He trusted his grandfather to make the right decisions and went along with them the way a sheep trusted its shepherd.

When he arrived on Earth, the meeting wasn't sched- uled for another twenty-four hours, so Hector retired to the room given him. He didn't know what his grandfather had told those who asked why he had requested a second room. He wasn't supposed to know, and when it was time, his grandfather would tell him.

What Hector knew, what his whole life had led to, was war.

Not the type of war Titans knew. He didn't know about going up skyscrapers, MechSuits in place, ready to destroy woefully unprepared enemies. He didn't know the war they taught in the Commonwealth's Institutes since his grandfather had not sent him there. Hector didn't know the wars that took place in space between fleets, at least not yet, though his grandfather had mentioned that would come soon.

Hector knew the type of war that took place on a battlefield. He knew wars where sometimes you had to sleep partly in the carcass of your enemy because the night was growing too cold to survive otherwise. Hector knew what it was like to stick a decapitated head on a post and do it one hundred more times, lining a road so that any who dared come that way knew the type of opposition they would meet.

Hector de Gracilis knew war in many ways, but really only in one. Winning mattered above all else. To lose even a single battle would be to lose one's dignity, respect, and perhaps even one's soul. He had no women to love, no brothers to share camaraderie with. Hector had only war, and it was a life he was more than satisfied with.

There are places in the Solar System that have been terraformed but are unexplored. The rivers that flow through the dense forests sometimes leak beneath the surface of the river basin. The water flows down to underground caves unknown by man or beast, and there they form pools. Over centuries, tiny fish have evolved within these pools. They're white and blind, having never seen light. They are content in their pools with their blind bodies, having no knowledge of anything else.

Hector de Gracilis, in his way, was a lot like those fish. His pool was war. His knowledge was bloodshed and victory.

When he retired to his room, he read a biography written two hundred years after the first Ascendant's passing. Hector understood that a lot of this history had been whitewashed by the man, but his genius couldn't be denied. Never before and never since had anyone done anything resembling what he'd accomplished.

For three hours, he delved into the book.

The knock on the door snapped him out of his focus.

"It's a weary old man, Hector. Let me sit with you for a few moments."

Hector put the book down and moved to the door. He waved his hand at the panel on the right, and the door opened, revealing his grandfather Caius. The two embraced and Hector pulled a chair over to the reclining seat he'd been lounging on. He sat in it to show his grandfather the proper respect.

"I know you've read that before," Caius said, pointing at the discarded book.

"A few times. I figured this being my first time on Earth, I should give it another ago."

Caius pulled out a small black orb from his tunic's pocket. He pressed a button on top, and a green light flashed on around its edge.

"It's a small StealthBlanket. It'll ensure that anyone who tries to listen to us will hear an extremely boring conversation." He placed the small orb on the table the book lay on. "Tomorrow you'll meet the first Ascendant's lineage, and I wanted to discuss what you can expect and what is expected of you."

"Of course," Hector answered.

Caius leaned back in his chair. The man was still strong and capable and had he sat in front of anyone except Hector, he would have appeared a formidable adversary. In front of Hector, he looked like a tired old man.

"Once we leave for the meeting, I cannot hide you any longer. You will be noticed. People will remember a man of your size and appearance. It's important, Hector, that you do not show that you know they notice, though you will know. Your eyes should be forward the entire time, and when we sit with the Ascendant and the Propraetors, you should be silent until called on to speak."

"I understand," Hector responded.

Caius nodded. "Yes, of course. I knew you would. Now, they are going to ask who you are, and they are going to suspect you've been modified. Some might call you a mutant, though there will be no proof. I can deal with those accusations, and you must show no anger. When it is your time to speak, all you are to do is to profess your loyalty to the Commonwealth and the Imperial Ascendant. You should go and kneel before the man. Let him touch your head or shoulders or whatever it is that he does. Those things aren't important, Hector. We are entering a dangerous time for you and me because no one can look at you or know I have kept you hidden for all these years and not wonder if I don't have ulterior motives."

Caius met Hector's eyes. The young man knew what he meant. While those fish didn't understand why they lived in that pool and could not see, Hector did understand why his life was nothing but war.

"We are beginning the endgame, my grandson. There is a new element thrown in, this Titan who conquers worlds, but I don't think he'll be a match for you. If we beat him, we will rise. The other Propraetors, even the Ascendant, they've all grown weak. Perhaps I've grown weak."

Hector opened his mouth to argue, but Caius waved him off.

"Yes, I'm sure I have grown weak, as wealth and power will make a man do. You, though. You have remained strong, and while I might be biased, I believe you grow stronger with each passing year. You're the reason the original Ascendant did what he did—so men like you could rule, creating safety for the weak. Tomorrow those who can only wish for the throne will meet the man who will one day take it. Remember, insults are nothing to the gods, and you are as close to them as any human I've ever met. Bow, perform the rituals, and let us make it to the coming war. After that, no human in the Solar System will deny you your rightful spot."

Hector went to his knees then, and although Caius tried to protest, the young man's strong voice shut the older man down.

"Thank you, Grandfather, for what you've made me and the opportunities before me." He bowed his head at Caius' knees. "I won't disappoint you."

"I know you won't. Now, up, up! Grovel tomorrow. Your loyalty to me needs no demonstration. Your life lived has proven it more than enough times."

The morning of the fateful meeting, Caius found he was nervous. He didn't feel like a traitor, though some might call him that in the future. He had always been loyal to the Commonwealth, and his coming act was nothing more than him showing that loyalty. The Commonwealth was never about one man. It was about "One People. One Purpose."

The present-day leaders were weak, and that was why this Titan could threaten an entire civilization.

No, Caius wasn't a traitor. He was the most loyal servant the Commonwealth had ever known. He'd sacrificed two lives—three if his own was included—to ensure that those who led the Commonwealth were fit to do so.

The nerves stemmed from the danger, and there was no way to avoid it. After the meeting today, the de Gracilis name would be known as a contender for the Ascendancy. Certainly, no one considered Alexander's son a possible heir. The man was in his mid-twenties and feckless. Everyone sitting around that table had to know that the family who performed the best in the coming war would assume the Ascendancy.

Perhaps there would be other surprises in the room today, though from everything Caius knew, none like his.

His main worry was whether the Ascendant would make an attempt on his or Hector's life before the war. It would certainly come into de Finita's mind. Not doing so might lead to the fall of his family's empire. Doing so might lead to the fall of the entire empire.

If an attempt did occur, Caius and Hector would probably survive. The odds weren't great, but he put them at better than fifty-fifty.

Yet, as Caius dressed for the meeting, he hoped the Ascendant was as loyal to the Commonwealth as he was. He hoped the man had enough honor to let the strongest hold the throne.

Otherwise, war might break out before the Titan returned home, and that would be very costly.

Alexander de Finita's face showed nothing. He saw a young man, monstrous in size, his presence like that of a god of war, but he didn't let his face show that he'd seen him. He didn't even glance in the young man's direction as he sat behind Caius.

No one in this room was a fool, though, of the seven Propraetors, some lacked the strict training afforded Alexander. Their faces showed their thoughts.

Alexander didn't need to ask a single question to understand what Caius' plan had been all along. He'd known the man's son, the perfect politician Caius had molded him into.

So, it was a two-pronged approach from the beginning, Caius? One would be the politician and one the warrior, but the politician is dead, so here you sit with this giant behind you. He wanted to smile but didn't. It would have been less obvious if Caius had sent a batch of poison to Alexander.

He would have to deal with this later because it was necessary to remind those here who sat upon the throne.

The table in front of him stretched from one end of the

room to the other in a rectangular shape, and he sat at the head. Three Propraetors were on one side, four on the other, each with a second in command sitting behind them.

A glass of water was in front of each of the Propraetors. None were drinking anything stronger yet, though Alexander imagined it might happen later. He wouldn't partake, of course, *especially* not after seeing the monster behind Caius.

Alexander stood up, his purple robe hanging down to his feet.

His voice was strong and sure. Caius might think he had the upper hand, but Alexander had not lived this long without playing the game well.

"You all know why you're here. The ex-Titan, Alistair Kane, is amassing an army, and his intention is clear: to come back here and destroy what has held humanity together for the past thousand years."

He gestured at the Propraetors.

"It is up to us to stop him. You seven represent the greatest families humanity has to offer. There has not been a credible revolution since the Commonwealth came into being. We are the protectors of humanity. We are the wall that holds back barbarians and democracy. These things, as we all know, brought humanity nuclear war." He paused and looked down at the table. "That must never happen again."

He looked up, and his eyes sought those of each person at the table.

"Today will be a day of strategy. We must cooperate since this traitor is growing powerful. I don't say that to scare you, but to prepare you. Is he ready now? No. From what I've been told, a vast army of cutthroats has flown out to kill him. Will he survive the attack? I have thought the man dead too many times to count him deceased once more. If he does survive, he will come out of it stronger and more capable."

He looked behind the Propraetors at their Consillariuses. He didn't let his eyes linger long on any of them.

"This is the first time many of you have traveled to Earth. Your presence as Consillariuses is nearly as important as the men and women you serve. I depend on you almost as much as your leaders to defend the Commonwealth. Your time for battle and glory will come."

Alexander motioned to the servants standing in the doorway. DataTracks were carried out and placed in front of each of the Propraetors. They lit up once the last one was set down.

"While I know you are all studious men and women and have no doubt taken the time to learn about our common enemy, I have prepared a guide for you. In front of you, you will see biographies, physical aspects, known family, and other pieces of information about those who wish us death."

A hologram of an old woman appeared in front of everyone.

"For too long, this woman has been shrouded in secrecy," Alexander continued. "She is called the AllMother, and legend has it she is my relation. I cannot say whether that is true or false, not with certainty, but I will hide nothing from you gentlemen and ladies. She may be a thousand years old, possessing mutant abilities never seen since. Or she may be a fraud. Either way, she is the spiritual leader of this insurrection."

The hologram switched to a giant of a man. The image was one of the last taken on the dreadnought Alistair Kane had commandeered. He was cutting his way through Titans, his Whip and body moving like a deadly snake through a mass of people.

"This is the physical leader. You know his name. You know he let Subversives go during his time as a Titan. You see him now as a mutant, his red eyes shining through the darkness of that ship. He's the one who will come for you, for your families, for everything we hold dear."

Alexander took a step back from the table.

"I'm going to leave you to study this information. I would like to meet with you individually over the next few hours." He smiled. "While there are refreshments to be had, please remember that we are all proper men and women here, and holding your alcohol until evening would benefit the Commonwealth. One People. One Purpose."

The room echoed the sentiment. "One People. One Purpose."

Alexander made his way around the table, shaking hands with the men and women who led the different planets of the Solar System. He reached Caius last, as he'd planned.

He shook the man's hand, leaned toward his ear, and whispered, "Would you and your Consillarius please visit me first, old friend?"

Alexander wasn't worried about the mutant or the man who had bred this creature. He had figured out a plan to deal with them. He, of course, would run it by the Fathers, but the plan seemed pretty solid to him.

Alexander led them to a smaller side room. The door opened for him as he reached it, and he entered. The table had food and drink on it. Two of his Praetorian Guard stood at attention in the back corners, and the two who had followed the group took up positions at the door.

Alexander looked at the guards in their MechSuits, wondering how they would fare against the mutant who had followed him here.

He took a seat at the round table, the one in between his guards, and gestured at the other two chairs. "Please, sit."

The mutant waited for Caius to take his seat, then followed suit. He had manners.

Alexander allowed himself to stare at the creature. He showed no emotion, but he didn't try to hide what he was looking at. By any standard, the man was huge, closer to the Biblical Sampson than any human Alexander had heard of. Even Kane's physical nature looked weak in comparison to this creature.

Without looking at the grandfather, Alexander asked, "When did you begin dabbling in modifications, Caius?"

Caius smiled. The young monster in front of Alexander showed no emotion.

"You hurt me, Alexander. My grandson's name is Hector, and his body is as pure as mine. There have been no modifications. It's good genes."

Alexander gave his attention to the older man. "True, he's missing the red eyes, but do you expect your Imperial Ascendant to believe someone that size is natural?"

Caius crossed one leg over the other, then rested his hands on his knees. He seemed at ease with these questions, no doubt because he knew they would come. "Come now, Alexander, there's no need to call me a liar." He gestured at the guards near the wall. "I'm sure if we were to comb through your endless supply of Titans or Praetorians, we would find some who are nearly the same size as my grandson. Don't forget what I once was. It isn't as if my genes are to be sneered at."

Alexander let his eyes fall on the beast again. This was Caius' play. This was his move to ascend to the throne. A long strategy, to say the least, and it made Alexander respect the man even more. He could relate to Caius' thirst for power. "Who do you serve, young man?"

There was no exaggeration in the beast's movements, nor any playfulness. Everything he did came off as sincere and honest. He stood, pushed his chair back slightly, and with a grace that his size said should be impossible, he walked to where the Ascendant sat. Hector de Gracilis knelt and bowed his head.

"It is my duty and my honor to serve the Commonwealth. I will do whatever the throne and my Imperial Ascendant request of me. One People. One Purpose."

Alexander didn't stand, but he did place a hand on the young man's head. "I am sure you will serve me well. Rise. There is much to talk about."

Hector did as he was told and returned to his seat.

A new idea came to Alexander. He would check something first and then continue with the rest of his plan. "Caius, I think your grandson will be a much-needed help to the current state of affairs. Would you mind me seeing how great of a warrior he is? A test, perhaps?"

Caius raised an eyebrow. "What kind of a test?"

Alexander shrugged as if it didn't matter. "I'd like to see him spar with one of my Titans."

Caius was quiet for a long moment. He looked at his hands resting on his knees. After a few seconds, he offered, "Why not two?"

The beast at his side showed no emotion.

The sparring round took place two hours later.

Caius approved everything beforehand. Alexander wanted him to feel good about this demonstration. He did not want the Propraetor to think this was an attempt on his grandson's life, though, of course, it was. Alexander had thought the suggestion of two Titans arrogant, so he had let the Titans know that their job was to kill this giant upstart in front of his grandfather.

Both Titans carried their Whips, and Caius approved them wearing MechSuits too.

The old man might be growing senile. That or this young man was even deadlier than his size suggested.

Alexander and Caius sat at the edge of the sparring room. It was a few kilometers from the building they'd originally met in. Alexander hadn't seen Hector since they'd agreed to this demonstration, and they were both waiting for the young man's arrival.

The two Titans stood on the left side of the room, ten meters separating them. Their Whips were holstered to their suits. Alexander hadn't picked them personally, but he knew they were battle-hardened, neither of them fresh out of the Institute.

When Alexander heard the man, he almost didn't believe his ears. The tunnel was to the right, and he could hear Hector's footsteps as he walked through it. The man sounded like some kind of elephant going to war, not a human.

Alexander's face showed nothing, and when he glanced at Caius, he saw no emotion there either. That wasn't training, though. The Propraetor was used to this.

Hector stepped out of the tunnel. He was large in the sense of planets, as if he should have his own gravitational pull. Alexander's eyes flashed to the Titans, and he couldn't be sure, but he thought their countenances changed—tightened up.

Hector looked like something from the time of the Romans, a gladiator reborn. He wore a short skirt-like piece of chainmail that covered his upper thighs, obviously to give him a greater range of movement. His broad chest was covered by a metal plate with the sign of House de Gracilis on it. He wore no armor on his arms, and his muscles bulged beneath the skin, making him look like a model of the human body to be used in a medical class.

Alexander could see two hilts sticking up from his back. His weapons.

"He's going to dual-wield?" Alexander asked.

Caius nodded.

He wore a metal helmet, one that showed his eyes and had a metal guard running down his nose.

He wore no other protection, while the men he faced were in MechSuits.

A voice came from a speaker above. "Your Imperial Ascendant, the second of the name Alexander de Finita, has asked you here to participate in a duel for his pleasure and edification. Do your best to serve your Ascendant. One People. One Purpose."

"ONE PEOPLE. ONE PURPOSE," all three contestants shouted in response.

The rules of a sparring match were simple: the opposite sides pressed until someone yielded. Most of the time, there would be some physical damage done, but that was easily patched up in the medical suites. Looking at Hector, the man Caius swore was not modified, Alexander wondered if he was insane.

He walked out onto the sparring field with almost no armor, planning on dual-wielding weapons, which was hard enough and nearly impossible when facing two enemies.

For sure, the man was monstrous. Moreover, energy rolled off him, as if each time his heart thumped inside his chest, those standing around him could feel it. It was like a furnace resided within him, its heat unable to be contained.

Hector walked forward. The two Titans spread farther apart to make each of them a harder target. Hector stopped in the middle of the sparring field. The Titans unleashed their Whips. Yellow and green lasers flowed down to the floor.

They approached the giant, who stood taller than either of them despite their MechSuits.

What came next, Alexander could barely keep up with.

The yellow Titan slashed his Whip in an almost playful gesture, something to open the sparring session up. Hector pointed his left finger at where the Whip ended, then his right hand went to the ground as if he were trying to perform a somersault.

The moment his hand touched down, his body lifted into the air in a line parallel to the ground, and he unleashed a flurry of kicks so quick that the Titan couldn't defend himself.

The warrior flew back five meters, hit the ground on his ass, and skidded farther. His MechSuit was dented.

Hector didn't slow for a second. His body moved in ways the laws of physics did permit, but only if his strength was unlike anything the Ascendant had ever seen. His right arm thrust him into the air, and his feet found the ground again. The second Titan swung his Whip from a lunge, giving him two meters of distance.

He wasn't trying to injure the beast but kill him, hoping to cut him in half.

Hector leaped, knees touching his chest, and cleared the swinging Whip. At that same moment, he pulled the weapons from his back, and Alexander lost the ability to hide his surprise.

His mouth opened.

His eyes widened.

The Titan tried to stand up, but compared to Hector, it

was like he moved underwater. The de Gracilis had strad-
dled his arm. With a twist of his knee, the Whip went
flying across the yard, dead. Lasers poured out of both
sides of the two hilts, and Hector brought the upper half to
the Titan's head. The lower lasers stretched, curving
beneath the Titan's arms and touching his back where his
lungs were. They tightened then, not allowing the Titan to
move his arms.

"Yield," Hector demanded.

The Titan turned his armored head to Alexander. He
gave a slight nod, and the Titan whispered, "Yield."

All of this had happened in seconds.

The first Titan was in the air, Whip slashing, trying to
overpower Hector.

It was as if he could feel the Titan's movements. He
turned, his dual lasers moving with him. With the left one,
he shielded himself from the Whip, and his right foot
slammed into the Titan's chest, the sound of bending metal
screeching throughout the sparring room.

Hector didn't waste a second. He leaped, following the
arc of the falling Titan, and was on him the moment he hit
the floor. He wrapped both hilt lasers around the man's
neck while the lower half bent to stab at where his heart
would be.

"Yield."

The Titan didn't even bother looking over. There was
no point. It was obvious that if you fought this man,
regardless of training, technology, or numbers, you'd die.

"Yield," the Titan said.

The lasers retracted into the hilts, and he slapped the
weapons into their places on his back. Hector straight-

ened, stepped over the Titan, and bowed to the two older men.

"One People. One Purpose," Hector bellowed.

Caius said nothing, only gave a short nod.

For the first time, Alexander saw the path to victory over this insurrection—and perhaps his path to his death.

It was late in the evening when the servant let Luna know the Imperial Ascendant wished to see her. After the last visit, she'd once again become a prisoner, though she had been allowed to send letters to her father. He'd written back quickly, and a regular correspondence had begun. It was her only outlet to the world, and while she feared the Ascendant's presence, she also craved human contact. Her servants, while always polite, would not speak to her in any real fashion. They had strict instructions to keep the relationship professional.

The letters she sent to her father were read and changed. The ones he sent back probably were manipulated in the same manner. He had asked if he could see her, if he could come to the Imperial Residence, and that the question had made it through let Luna know the Ascendant was planning a show for her father.

"Come, look and see, everything is fine here. Your daughter is merely helping us find her traitorous husband and is free to leave whenever she wishes."

Luna, without a doubt, would be expected to play along.

The servant was standing in her doorway. Luna was gazing at the letter she'd been composing.

"Ma'am?" the servant said.

"He wishes to see me now? At this hour?" Luna said without looking over. She didn't like this, despite her craving for human contact. Something wasn't right. Luna had seen the ships arrive in the Imperial Residence's private hangar. She didn't know who had come, but she knew they were important people. In the months she'd been here, she'd never seen anything of the sort.

"Yes," the servant replied. "That's his request. Ma'am, with all due respect, I would recommend you honor it."

Luna stood. "Of course I'm going to honor it. Please give me a few minutes to ready myself."

"Certainly," the servant said before stepping away from the door and letting it close.

Luna didn't do much as far as getting ready. She just tried to prepare herself mentally for what might come. Living here had become a horror, one she hadn't realized was possible. There'd been no contact with Alistair, not through the normal routes or whatever insanity she'd felt before. She didn't know where her husband was, what he was doing, or if there was any chance she'd ever see him again.

She'd given that one little speech to him, and after that, she'd been thrust away, given no more knowledge, and asked for nothing more.

If Allie wasn't still alive, she thought as she threw water on her face, *you wouldn't still be here.*

That was the only hope she had. She was still in this

hell, so Alistair had to be out there, still had to be some kind of threat.

The only thing she could do now was wait, even if it meant she had to wait in a prison. He would do the same for her. She knew that. Even if he wouldn't, she'd do it for him.

She turned the water off and left her quarters. The female servant was waiting for her, and they crossed the Residence toward the throne room.

When they were in front of the closed doors, the servant stepped aside, leaving Luna to enter on her own.

She walked past the Praetorian Guards on either side.

The double doors opened for her, and she stepped through the entryway. Alexander de Finita sat on his throne. Guards stood against the walls, their faces unreadable behind their metal armor.

Luna walked to the expected place in front of the throne and got down on both knees. She bowed her head. "How may I be of service, my liege?"

"One People. One Purpose, yes, Luna?"

"One People. One Purpose, my liege."

"Please, stand," the Ascendant directed, and Luna did so. The Ascendant considered her for a moment as if deciding something in his head. "The question continually comes up with you, Luna. How loyal are you to the Commonwealth?"

"My liege, I believe my actions indicate that my heart and soul are committed to the Commonwealth. To the throne as well."

Again the silent stare. He was considering something, and she hated the suspense. She knew it wouldn't be good.

"Things are happening now that you're not aware of. Even as we speak, your husband is gathering an army to return to our Solar System and attack the Commonwealth. Everything your family believes in and holds dear, he is planning on destroying. It won't just be *our* world he tries to destroy, but the other seven planets as well. A lot of people have died at his hand already, and I promise you, a lot more will."

Luna looked at her feet, doing her best to hide any emotion. She didn't think the Ascendant was lying; Alistair had to be out there, or she would have been discarded. An army, though? Wanting to destroy the entire Commonwealth? Those were the things she couldn't bring herself to believe. "How may I be of service, my liege? That is all I want at this point in my life—to help the Commonwealth grow stronger."

"You say those words, and to a degree, I believe you." The Ascendant nodded as he spoke the next few sentences. "Your actions do make me think you're with me. Staying here. The message to your husband. Understanding the need for secrecy. However, I've never been married. I don't know what that type of bond is like between two people. How strong is it? How far will one person go for the other?"

Luna looked up. "My bond with my husband broke when he traded in the Commonwealth. I have no allegiance to him."

The Ascendant smiled, and Luna saw her fate in it. A nasty end, something she wouldn't wish on her worst enemy.

"Luna, I would like you to marry another. A young man

from a family that rivals any but my own. His name is Hector, and your marriage to him will assure me of your allegiance to the Commonwealth and strengthen the Commonwealth in ways you can't understand."

It took all of Luna's concentration to not attack the man sitting before her. Not to rip his eyes from his skull.

All she could do if she wanted to live and have a chance of seeing Alistair again was say, "Whatever you wish, my liege."

CHAPTER EIGHT

The coming forces were no longer in the fourth dimension. Alistair didn't have to force his mind into the atmosphere, then across membranes that separated the dimensions to see those who were coming to kill him.

All he had to do was look at the sky.

The force was so vast that he could see them from thousands of kilometers away. They lit up the night sky like stars.

A week had passed since he first saw the armada. Every waking moment since then had been spent preparing for the battle. He'd enlisted everyone from his council down to the tribal leaders of the gigantes.

The only thing he was sure of was that they did not have enough men or firepower to stop the invaders.

The force had dropped into the third dimension a day ago, and Alistair's scanning equipment had been able to see everything that was coming for them. The Commonwealth had sent four dreadnoughts. There were twenty-five in the sky. They had stealth bombers that could enter the atmosphere from space, drop plasma, and return to the dreadnoughts to reload, thus keeping the dreadnoughts out of danger. Servia had spent a lot of time studying the force, and she thought, based on the shape of half the dreadnoughts, that they contained reinforced landing ships. That meant they could put boots on the ground, shoot back up to space, replenish the troops, and come down again. The dreadnoughts would not be harmed, and destroying the landing ships would be a problem.

The planet wasn't equipped for this type of warfare. Sure, they had drones that could burn hundreds of kilometers of land, but fighting armed forces like this? The corporation that had ruled before had relied on commerce, knowing they made too many people too much money to need state-of-the-art protection.

His people were, for lack of a better term, fucked.

Alistair couldn't think of a way out of it. He'd spent the last twenty-four hours alone, hoping something would come to him as it usually did when he had time to think. This time, nothing came. They didn't have the spider ships that they'd used back on Pluto, so they couldn't drill their way into one of the dreadnoughts. Their dreadnought would be blasted out of the sky if it attempted to rise out of the atmosphere.

There wasn't time to call the Terram.

He couldn't challenge the leaders to a duel.

Alistair had nothing.

He'd asked his council to sit outside with him. At the current speed and trajectory, the ships would land in twenty-two hours. Preparations continued while he thought, so nothing slowed down because of him, but he needed to tell those depending on his leadership that he was out of ideas.

They sat on one of the compound's garden terraces. The planet's two moons shone on either side of the sky, and between them, the new stars burned. They were bigger and brighter than they'd been the night before, and by tomorrow evening, they would be streaking through the atmosphere.

Thoreaux, Servia, Relm, Faitrin, Caesar, and the AllMother sat around a circular concrete table. Alistair had invited Nero, but the gigante hadn't shown up.

The night was cool but not cold. The AllMother wore a light sweater, and everyone else long sleeves except Caesar, who sported a cut-off shirt, more used to the planet's weather than anyone else at the table.

Alistair stared at the coming armada. "I don't have any ideas. I don't know how to stop what's coming. I've spent twenty-four hours thinking and trying to plan, and I have nothing. The only thing I know to do is something that will surely end with us dying, and that's to stand and fight. We will kill some of them. A lot of them, probably, but in the end, they will overrun us. If we could flee, I would, but we cannot. They will catch us, and at the expense of some of their army, kill us."

He was quiet for long seconds, staring at the first enemies he didn't know how to defeat.

"If anyone has any ideas, anything that might help, I'm open."

No one spoke for thirty seconds, then Servia said, "Do you think we can beat them?"

He nodded but pursed his lips. "Based on everything you've given me this past week, they're going to outnumber us three to one. They came to win and probably left their home planets open to attack because they've brought so many warriors."

Relm turned to Caesar. "The rocs? Is it possible to enlist them?"

It might have sounded like a stupid question to those who hadn't seen what Alistair had done, somehow communicating with an animal and forming a bond in the middle of battle. It wasn't a stupid question to Caesar, either. "I've sent envoys. It's hard to say what the rocs will do, but we've tried."

"Even so," Alistair interrupted, "they won't make up the difference." He looked at his council. "I know this will fall on deaf ears, but if you want to escape, now is the time. There are corvettes that can leave the planet within the next hour, and I doubt anything up there is going to chase you. I've already seen a few leave tonight, though I don't know who it was."

"I'd hit you right now if you weren't so damn dangerous," Relm stated.

The AllMother spoke, and it was obvious she spoke for the table. "No one's going anywhere, Prometheus. At least no one at this table. If that was what anyone here wanted, they wouldn't be here."

"I know," Alistair answered. He stood up, and Obs did as well, having been silent beneath the table the entire time. The drathe remained at his master's side. "We've got a little less than twenty-two hours before they land. Spend it with those you love, or spend it thinking about a way out of this. I'm open to any and all ideas. Tomorrow, we go to battle again."

"*Ave*, Prometheus," those at the table said in a whisper. Some were looking at the coming force, others were staring at their hands.

His despair, *their* despair, was palpable.

Alistair left the table, prepared to go back inside and wrack his brain until he came up with an idea or was forced to suit up for battle. He was nearly at the door of the compound when he realized Obs had stopped. He turned and saw the drathe looking at the AllMother, who was on his heels.

The rest of the council remained seated, none of them appearing to pay any attention to the old woman.

"You have a few minutes for me, Alistair?" she asked as she reached down to pat Obs on the head.

"Of course. Want to go to my quarters?"

She shook her head. "No. I have another idea. Would you mind following me?"

Obs turned to look at his master. Alistair raised both eyebrows. "By all means."

The AllMother led the way. They passed the table with the rest of his council. Relm gave him a questioning look and Alistair shrugged. He didn't know what this was about.

She led him about a kilometer away from the compound until they were standing alone in a large field that looked like it had once been used for some kind of sports. There were little balls here and there, though the grass was high. The AllMother stopped in the middle and turned to look at him for the first time since she had started walking.

"Prometheus, I'm going to show you something, and you're going to have to trust that it won't weaken me to the point of no return. Do you understand?"

"No, not really."

"Obs," the AllMother said, "would you go wait for us at the edge of the field?"

The drathe barked and trotted away without looking at Alistair. "I think he would trade me for you in a heartbeat."

The AllMother quickly rolled her eyes. "The animal would rip my heart out to ensure yours kept beating. I'm going to give you another piece of advice before I show you what I brought you here for. Keep him by your side during this coming battle. I have a feeling you'll need him."

Alistair looked at Obs, who was staring at him. He'd kept the drathe away from battles of late, partly because of terrain, partly because he loved the animal as much as life itself. He didn't want anything to happen to him. "Okay." He turned back to the AllMother. "Why are we here?"

"I'm going to attack you, Prometheus. Not as hard as I can since I don't want you severely hurt before tomorrow, but I'm not going to take it easy, either. I want you to fend me off."

Alistair chuckled. "You're serious right now?"

Her eyes narrowed and her brow furrowed. "Don't forget what happened to the three Myrmidons who tried to abduct me back on Pluto. I wonder if they chuckled before I broke their bodies in half?"

Alistair's laughter died. He remembered well the legs

that had broken just because she'd willed it. "What if I hurt you?"

"That's the whole point, boy. I want to see you try."

The old lady walked two meters and raised her hand, palm out. She brought it back to slap him, but Alistair's hand caught her wrist in the air. He didn't press hard, only stopped her from making contact.

Their eyes met. "You'll have to do better than that," he said.

"Okay." The words came from behind him, and a hand slapped him across the face.

Alistair released the AllMother as Prometheus tried to roar to the front of his mind, the unseen attack bringing out the killer. Alistair forced his other side away but quickly backed up.

He saw two AllMothers, both looking the same.

He felt the leg that kicked him but found himself—perhaps for the first time—too shocked to react. He fell on his ass.

Alistair looked at the third AllMother. He didn't understand how it was possible, but he didn't have time because the fourth's foot kicked him in the back of the head.

Alistair rolled, knowing he had to get away from whatever in hades was happening if he were going to have a chance of figuring out how to stop it. He popped up on his feet and looked at the four in front of him.

The whisper came from right next to his ear. "Hello."

Her hands hit him with flat palms, and he knew then she was using more than muscles. The former Titan rose into the air as if thrown by a gigante. He soared four meters before landing on his back and skidding through the tall grass.

Alistair didn't wait then but kipped up and dropped into a crouch. He quickly spun three hundred and sixty degrees, checking all sides before looking at the growing number across the field.

More came into being every few seconds. They weren't there, and then they were.

The group started walking toward him.

"I don't want to hurt you!" Alistair called.

"*Try.*"

The word came from both sides of his head, and he felt four hands grab him. They tossed him as if he were little more than a child.

Alistair found himself once again in the air, and this time he would land between fifteen or twenty of the AllMothers.

Replicas, he thought.

He tucked his body and rolled. He kept the roll short, bouncing up and attacking the first AllMother he saw. He swung an elbow at her stomach but watched as its permanence disappeared in a cloud of fading dust.

He turned to attack the next one but caught an elbow in his face. Blood burst from his lips and dripped down his chin.

He couldn't hold back the warrior then. Prometheus burst forward, and all he cared about was stopping this charade.

His speed increased, and gone was the fear of hurting the AllMother. Replicas fell to the left and right and he attacked, kicking, punching, head-butting—whatever was necessary to decrease their number.

Still more came. Somehow, every time he dispatched one, two replaced them. The old woman's speed shouldn't have been possible. Prometheus continued to push forward to cut through as many replicas as he could, yet the blows rained down on him, bruising his unprotected body and causing his ears and nose to bleed.

He couldn't stop them all.

There were too many.

In the distance, he heard Obs whine.

Prometheus knelt as the blows continued. Using all his strength, he flung himself into the air, using his mind to propel him higher than he'd usually be able to go.

He shed the clinging replicas of the AllMother and did a backflip over the rest, then landed on his knee and looked up at them. He knew they would be on him again in seconds, and soon he'd have to tell them to stop. Tell *her* to stop because she was going to injure him.

No, he thought. *What is she teaching me here? What am I supposed to learn?*

It came to him, and he understood.

Kill the shepherd, and the sheep will scatter.

There was only one of her. The rest were just her mind playing its tricks—a powerful mind, yes, perhaps the most powerful to ever exist, but still only a mind.

Where was the real one?

Pro's eyes scanned the oncoming crowd, knowing that more were appearing around him. It didn't matter. None of them did.

Kill the shepherd, and the sheep will scatter.

He saw it, then. The smallest smirk—the only thing that marked her out from the rest, who stared with dead, empty eyes.

Prometheus barreled forward. Replicas came at him, but he lowered his shoulder, and his muscular legs shoved him forward.

He was on her in seconds, and he didn't let up. He grabbed her by the throat and thrust her into the air. The old woman's hands came up to his arm as the rest fell away, turning into that fading dust.

The fear he saw in her eyes forced Prometheus away, letting Alistair return.

He set her on the ground and took his hand off her throat. "Are you okay?"

The old woman rubbed her throat as she smiled at her protégé. "Yes. For a second there, I thought I might have overdone it once you grabbed me." With her free hand, she brought his face closer to hers and checked his bloody lip and busted nose. "They'll be sore, but you'll live. You might want to stop by the med center before tomorrow morning to see if they can give you anything to take the swelling down."

She stepped back.

"You're a hard man to teach, Alistair. You're wise, but sometimes you forget what you know. Do I need to say anything else, or has this lesson done enough to show you?"

He smiled, and his face hurt as he did. "This was enough. I don't think any other words are necessary."

The AllMother looked past Alistair at the drathe. "Sorry about that, Obs. I'll let you take care of him now. Make sure he gets someone to look at his wounds, and don't forget that you're to go with him tomorrow."

Obs barked, then came in a fast trot to meet his master.

The two of them watched the old woman walk away, still rubbing her neck.

CHAPTER NINE

Cristin de Monaham looked at the planet she planned to burn. She hated this planet, though she had not told anyone that. Cristin, a warlord in her own right, rarely told anyone anything she was thinking. This planet, with its lush forests and warm sun, was very different from the one she'd grown up on. To Cristin, this planet was the stuff of legend. Things her father had talked to her about when she was a child, the places she would conquer and the worlds she and her children would inherit.

At thirty-eight years old, Cristin had no children, and the only world she owned was the one made of ice that her father had handed down.

She had been told that life would be different, and it wasn't until she grew to womanhood that she realized her father had been a foolish man in many ways. One of them was how easy he imagined the future would be. He had forgotten what everyone else on their home planet knew: life was not easy, and anything one wanted would have to be taken by blood and steel.

Cristin learned that lesson early when her father died and she was thrust into a war that would last too many years and cost too many lives. Well, perhaps not *too* many; when the war was finished, her position had been solidified both on her planet and off it. The lives had been well spent because the war had created a myth about Cristin de Monaham.

The Ice Queen.

Now she flew toward a man that she thought was worthy of more bloodshed. Defeating him would expand her empire, and with it, her family's security.

That was the one thing her father had been right about —family. The rest of the universe could burn, along with everyone in it, but one had to watch out for one's lineage.

The two men Cristin flew with were inconsequential. She had kept the peace established after their war because it had been profitable to do so. Now it was profitable to use their war machines to defeat this—

Cristin grew a bit hazy when trying to classify this man. He was a mutant, though she had no quarrel with that. What was he fighting for, though? Why had he come to this planet to free the gigantes? Cristin didn't mind him doing that; her business competed with this planet's.

Still, the question of why plagued her.

Her reason for everything she did was her family, the one that had made their home on a cold, desolate planet but had managed to thrive generation after generation.

Why was he here? Why was he freeing creatures that had no business being freed?

Cristin wasn't sure if she would get answers to those questions. She hadn't come this far to palaver with the mutant. No, she'd come here to get what her father had promised her: a warm planet.

One of the other warlords she traveled with, Simo de Colombus, was introduced through the mic in her ear.

"Simo would like to speak with you, Queen," the AI said.

"Put him through."

"Why are we going so slow?" the man demanded with no greeting.

Cristin had set the pace for the entire voyage, and now she'd slowed down. "I wanted to get a look at the planet."

"Why? Have you not seen enough of it in holovids?"

These men would never understand. They came from warm planets, from places with forests and rivers that flowed without ice covering the first meter of them. They couldn't understand what it meant to her and her family to finally *earn* what so many others had been given.

"We will be there shortly, Simo. Our scouts say they don't have the defenses to stop us even if we took a year to make it there."

"Simo has ended communications, Queen," the AI said.

Never mind him, Cristin thought. "Connect me to Galer."

"Yes, Queen."

A second went by, then the fat man's loud voice was in Cristin's ear. "Simo messaged you complaining, I take it?"

"Yes," Cristin responded.

"Me too. He's not happy with the pace. I told him to calm down, enjoy the ride, he's going to have fireworks soon. He didn't want to listen."

The fat man talked too much. He told everyone what

was in his head at all times, which was an extremely foolish thing to do.

"Are you going to the ground, Galer?" she asked.

"Me? Why would I do such a thing? We've got all the weapons and tools we need to stay up here, watch fireworks, and go down when it's all finished. I was thinking of smoking some of that good Zeus' grass I got on your planet while I watch it." He paused for a moment. "Wait. Are you planning on going there?"

Cristin didn't want to answer yet. "I'm not sure. I was curious what your plans were."

"I plan to eat and be merry while my soldiers bring me a planet. I suggest you do the same. No need for crazy antics, Ice Queen."

Cristin ended the connection. She looked at the panels hanging from the ceiling of her bridge and her twenty pilots harmonized with the dreadnought.

That had been the difference between her and these two men in their war those many years ago. *They* had let their soldiers fight for them, and she had fought *with* her soldiers. Her family had been the weakest of the three when the war started, and now she dictated the pace to the two men.

If she sat here with them, she might lose her edge. If she went down with her people, no one could take away what she'd earned.

For Cristin de Monaham, death wasn't a possibility. Perhaps it was her father's words when she was a young girl, telling her what she would have and how much she would expand their empire. Perhaps it was only her belief in herself.

In the end, it didn't matter. She would not die on this planet, and to remain on this ship and watch from on high was not something an Ice Queen would do. Those born in warmth could afford that.

Those born in the cold took with blood and steel.

CHAPTER TEN

Alistair watched as the first ships breached the atmosphere. They were distant, nearly at the planet's curvature, but he could see their fiery blaze as they sliced through the sky.

They did what he feared they would. They had brought incendiaries with them, and he could see them beginning to burn the ripe forests that housed so many gigantes and so much wildlife. Caesar had been working on bringing as many of the gigantes as possible to the city. It was the only place they had ground-to-air support.

Many of the gigantes had listened, but Alistair refused to command them as slaves, so some had remained in their homes.

Alistair's advanced eyes could see the flames starting to catch. He wouldn't look away, even though he wanted to. Any death that happened here was his fault, no one else's. The AllMother had been right. He'd taken his eyes away from their end goal, and death was coming for people beyond his inner circle. For *beings* beyond his inner circle, because even the beautifully hued trees and shrubs would burn.

Alistair stood watching on a hill on the edge of the city. His transport was behind him, and he'd heard Servia's land moments ago. He knew he had to get back and ready himself for war, but he wanted to see this first. Someone needed to witness the first burning of the planet that had been peaceful before he arrived, or at least peaceful for some. Certainly, the death of all who lived here hadn't been a possibility.

Servia came to his side. "*Ave*, Prometheus. All simulations show they're going to wipe out the land beyond the city first. There are ships just beyond the curvature that are starting to burn the opposite way. In ten to twelve hours, the world will be on fire. Then they're going to make their way here."

"It's the smart move. Destroy any chance of an attack coming from behind." Alistair looked at his transport, the side door still open.

"The city is as fortified as we can make it. As many gigantes as we could persuade are inside the walls. It will be harder for them to burn the city. They'll have to put boots on the ground."

Alistair knew all this; he also knew Servia was trying to get him to do something—anything—besides stare at the destruction.

Kill the shepherd, Alistair thought. He looked at the sky. The dreadnoughts were visible in the daylight, hovering just outside the atmosphere, their lights burning brightly.

I just gotta get the damned shepherd down here, and then I'll scatter her entire fucking flock.

He started walking toward the transport, calling as he did, "I'm suiting up. Get me the fastest transport you have, hook Jeeves up to the thing, and put every weapon you have on it."

Alistair didn't wait for Servia to respond. He hopped into the transport and pulled into the sky.

Servia watched the transport take off, processing what she'd been told to do.

She wasn't sure what he was planning on doing, but she didn't care much.

Guilt had frozen Prometheus. She understood it, or at least why he felt it. He'd come here and conquered the planet, and now they all might die because of that decision.

Guilt was an acceptable response, at least in the beginning.

Now, though? With the enemy at the gates, bringing more firepower than she or anyone else knew how to handle?

The time for guilt was over. The time for action had arrived. Servia had seen no way out of this for the past week. Before that, she'd been neck-deep in the administrative work Pro had given her. It'd been his duty to guide them, but now there wasn't anything to guide.

He had to rescue them.

As Servia watched the transport fly toward the compound, she didn't allow herself to smile. There was no time for smiling and barely time to consider her orders.

However, for the first time in a week, she allowed herself to hope.

They called him Prometheus all the time, but everyone who'd seen him in battle knew there were two sides to the man: the thoughtful, loving, and currently guilt-ridden leader known as Alistair Kane, and the warrior who knew no limits, held no discussions, and killed without feeling known as Prometheus.

Servia allowed herself to hope because it hadn't been Alistair Kane who'd left this hill. It had been the only god of war she'd ever met.

Ave, Prometheus.

"Sir," Jeeves said, "I feel it's my duty to let you know that the odds of you being killed in this endeavor are greater than eighty percent. I also feel it's my duty to tell you that if you want someone to die with you so you're not alone, I am not the entity you need. I will not die but simply remain at the compound."

"Jeeves, if you don't shut up, once I'm done with them, I'm going to come back and kill you," Alistair said.

"Point taken, sir," the AI responded. "All systems are go. Ready when you are."

Alistair looked at the controls in front of him. He'd flown these things before, but rarely, and not in combat missions. "Jeeves, before shutting up completely, how well-trained are you in corvettes?"

Jeeves answered, "I'd say about as well-trained as you are. I'll primarily be able to assist by detecting things you don't see and letting you know how close you are to death."

Alistair nodded. "All right, Jeeves. Let's do this." Obs was in a small seat that folded out of Alistair's. He'd taken it to heart when the AllMother had told him to keep Obs with him, and he wasn't leaving the drathe out of this one.

For the drathe's part, his hair stood on end, and he wouldn't stop whining. Alistair ignored him as he touched the glass panels in front of him, firing up the corvette's engines. The machine launched straight into the air, going much higher than he'd intended.

"I would advise a lighter touch," Jeeves said.

"Remember what I said about shutting up?"

"Of course, sir. We are currently five hundred kilometers from the nearest ship. We can get there in—"

Alistair turned the thrusters, and the ship ripped forward. "Turn the ship transparent."

The walls appeared to fade, allowing him to see everything around him instead of only what was in front. He pulled up to clear the city's wall. A few minutes after that, the strangely colored plants beneath blurred together as the ship sped forward. He didn't know how fast he was going, only that the enemy Jeeves had talked about was now visible.

Obs whined louder.

"Hush, Obs! Jeeves, you gotta tell me when I'm within firing range."

"I advise you to turn around, sir."

"Advise me when to fire this godsdamn weapon."

"Yes, sir."

Slowly this time, Alistair faded into the back of the

shared mind and the warrior came forward. Death became a thing that only happened to others, and it was a condition he was glad to deliver.

The ship raced through the air, time disappearing for Pro. His eyes focused on the first enemy, and his mind no longer cared that he wasn't in his element.

Death was what mattered.

"In firing range," Jeeves said.

Prometheus glanced at the glass panel. It changed slightly, giving him the ability to fire in front of him. The other ship was turning around, knowing that someone was coming for it. Fire blazed beneath them.

Pro started firing.

"Take over flying. Get me as close to it as you can."

Jeeves said nothing, but the controls to either side of Pro began moving in different directions.

Lasers sliced above and below the enemy.

He fired back. Pro's ship rocked downward hard—much too hard, but they dodged the incoming laser. Prometheus said nothing, only tried to straighten himself as Jeeves straightened the ship.

"Obs, you there?"

The animal gave a half-yelp, half-bark response, and that was enough for Pro.

They were close to the fire now, and the enemy had the advantage of higher altitude. Prometheus' head was on a swivel, trying to find the other ship.

"Get me a godsdamn vision of him," he cursed.

Jeeves lifted the ship, turning almost vertical. Prometheus tilted his head in what normally would be the up position.

The ship was coming straight toward him and firing.

"HIGHER!" he shouted, and the thrusters threw him back against the chair when Jeeves pushed the ship as fast as it could go. The lasers barely missed the lower half. Jeeves started turning again and Prometheus was upside-down, but he could use the corvette's weapons. He started firing, laser after laser pouring from the side of the ship.

The enemy wove in and out, the pilot much more skilled than Prometheus had thought possible.

He didn't see the laser that hit the ship, only felt it as they were knocked off-course.

"We're going down, sir," Jeeves said. "Trying to land, but there's no way to continue flying."

Prometheus looked behind him and saw flames stretching up the side of the ship. The lasers had not hit home but had started a fire.

The last thing he remembered seeing was the fire on the ground beneath him heading directly for them.

CHAPTER ELEVEN

Thoreaux stared at the holovid in front of him, unable to believe what he'd just seen.

Prometheus had flown into battle, as brazen and arrogant as ever. He'd watched the dogfight, and the entire thing had taken only a few minutes. In that short time, Thoreaux had seen his leader overmatched, unable to maneuver or fire.

Then he watched the man he followed—the man he loved like a brother—take a hit and fall into the flames.

He stared silently, along with the rest of Pro's council. His eyes were wet as tears threatened to fall.

"What just happened?" Relm asked. "I didn't see that, did I?"

For so long, they had seen Prometheus rise and rise again. No one watching the dogfight could believe he'd lost. It didn't seem possible.

"Is he..." Servia began to say, but her voice trailed into silence before she could speak the word they were all thinking.

Dead.

Thoreaux reached up and roughly wiped away his tears. "Jeeves? Is he alive? Is Prometheus *alive?*"

The AI spoke over the intercom. "I cannot say. The wreck destroyed my connection with the ship."

"Give me a prediction, then," Thoreaux ordered through clenched teeth.

"I did the best I could to land smoothly. The ship was upside-down and the AI implant was on the top, so it was immediately destroyed. Based on where the corvette was hit, the speed, trajectory, impact velocity, and environment around the crash—"

"Give me a percentage," Thoreaux demanded.

"Five to fifteen percent chance he's alive. His modifications might push it as high as seventeen percent, though the confidence level falls dramatically at that point."

Thoreaux leaned forward, placed his hands on the table, and looked down. He was quiet for a long moment, using everything in him to keep from shedding the tears that wanted to flow.

When he looked up, his eyes weren't dry, but the tears were still at bay. He found the AllMother sitting to his right, Caesar between them. "Can you see him?"

The AllMother stared at the holovid, flames filling it. She was deep in concentration, obviously trying to do what Thoreaux asked.

A full minute passed, and she shook her head. "I don't see him anywhere." She met Thoreaux's eyes. "I'm not strong, though. You all heard what I did with him last night, and I'm only awake out of sheer adrenaline. He could still be alive."

"What do you think?" Thoreaux asked, still leaning on the table.

"I think we need to prepare this city for battle. If he is alive, he will handle himself."

Thoreaux nodded a few times, trying to force his emotions away. Faitrin was two people over, next to Servia, and he couldn't look her in the eyes right now. He would cry.

"Caesar, prepare the troops. Servia, prepare the land-to-air retaliation. Once they finish with the forest, they'll come here."

Alistair opened his eyes. He could hear something in the distance, though he had no idea what it was. He blinked a few times, unable to understand why he could only see white.

Am I blind?

The next question that came to mind was, why couldn't he move? His arms, legs, torso—everything was stuck in one place.

Am I paralyzed?

He wiggled his fingers and toes, pushing the paralyzation theory out and making him realize what surrounded him. Past events came back to him, and he remembered seeing the fire as the corvette fell into it.

He was surrounded by some sort of foam, probably flame-retardant material. Jeeves hadn't wrecked the damned ship but had somehow achieved a landing that didn't kill or break the thing.

Alistair could have kissed the intelligence on the mouth had it had one and had he been able to move.

He didn't understand the noise he heard. It was like a low whistle.

He also didn't know if he could get out of this foam. His hands were in his lap, his legs close together; he had no leverage.

Slowly, he started to move his arms and legs. Pushing both at the same time, he rocked back and forth, creating small spaces within the foam. With each rock, he created more room for his muscles to work.

It took him about five minutes, but finally, he had enough space to kick.

The foam shot out of the ship and went ten meters into the air before crashing into...

"That's not possible," he said aloud as he stared at ash instead of flames. How long had he been out? Long enough for the fires to burn out? If that was true, then the city was lost, Thoreaux and the council were dead, and the movement—

A giant head filled the space he was staring at. Not a *giant* head, but a *giant's* head.

It was Nero.

"I was wondering when you would wake. I've been out here an hour, keeping the fire at bay. Tough work." He smiled and raised a canister to the hole. "I stole it from the city." He tapped his temple with his free hand. "Saw that you would act stupidly, so prepared early. Come. Get out. There's much to do."

A look of confusion grew on the gigante's face.

"I saw the drathe in my dream. Is he here?"

Oh, gods, Alistair thought, panicked. Adrenaline flooded his muscles and he stood up, destroying the foam around him. He turned to the seat behind him and started to rip into the foam there, pulling huge chunks off and throwing them with abandon.

On the third pull, a dark shape shot out of the foam, pushing Alistair back and landing on top of him.

Obs' tongue flashed out, and Alistair got slobber all over his face.

"*OBS!*" he shouted, reaching up to grab the damned animal. He overpowered the drathe, pulling him close, and Obs tilted his head toward Alistair's chin to continue licking.

They were now outside the ship, lying on ash, with a gigante standing above them. At that moment, Alistair didn't care what else was happening in the universe. "I'm sorry, I'm sorry, I'm sorry," he repeated in a rush.

Finally Nero stepped in, dropped a giant hand on the back of Obs' neck, and lifted him by the scruff. He set him down quickly and Obs turned his head, confused by everything around him.

"Sorry, Obs. There is no time for cuddling. There is much work to be done, and the three of us are meant to do it."

Alistair slowly sat up, looking around. The fire was a half-kilometer away in all directions. "Where in hades did you hide, Nero?"

"Same place as always." He stomped his right foot. "Underground. I spent the last week building and hoping this was the right place. Dreams are directionally right but not always accurate, right?"

Alistair didn't know or care. He stood up, understanding what the sound had been. Hundreds of those canisters lay around the ship, and when Alistair examined the giant, he saw soot covering him.

No human could have done this. Only the technology inside a gigante could have protected and healed him long enough to *start* putting out the flames and create enough space that they could be safe.

The AllMother's words came back to him.

All the while, a great wind carries me across the sky.

Alistair didn't know if the gods existed, and he felt certain that if they did, they didn't interfere in human life, yet something seemed to be in play here.

He stood up and brushed the remaining foam off him, then looked around again. The flames farther out were dying, and he knew that meant the enemy was moving closer to the city.

"We've got to get back," he said as his eyes narrowed, looking across the distance at the massive place he'd come from.

The gigante shook his head. "No. We're not to go back. We're to wait here."

Alistair whipped around. "What are you talking about?"

"The dream says we wait here. So we wait."

Alistair had to look up to view the giant's face. There was no humor in it, no levity. He was serious and sounded insane.

"I can't wait *here*," Alistair said. He pointed at the planet's only city. "They need me. They need us. If we wait here, they'll all die."

The gigante looked at the sky. "No, spaceman. If we go

back, they die. If we stay here, they have a chance of living. It is a small chance, I'll give you that, but any chance is better than none, right?"

Alistair didn't know what he was looking at. There was only the enemy up there, and the chances of them looking in this little clearing were small. What could they do here? Nothing. The trek back would take far too long. Alistair would have to think of something, but staying here was not an option.

"Nero, I'm eternally grateful that you saved me, but Obs and I are getting out of here. Nearly everything I care about is back in that city, and that's where I'm going."

The giant sighed as if he were trying to explain something to a small and not very bright child. "If you leave, they will die. If you stay, they might live." His language was stilted, and at best, communication with the gigantes wasn't easy. Right now, it was nearly impossible.

"Why didn't I dream then, Nero? Last time, I had the dream. Why didn't I this time?"

Nero shrugged, his head still turned to the sky. "We are all the heroes of our own story. In the real world, though, there are different heroes at different times. Now is not your time. Now is mine. Do not be greedy, spaceman."

Cristin was in her quarters in the dreadnought slowly making its way to the main city. To Simo's chagrin, the pace she'd set was the fires' pace. She would arrive at the same time as the flames, then their armies would drop down and finish off this planet.

She was dressing for battle. She wore the ice armor of her planet and her family. It was white, shielding her from her head to her feet, just as ice covered every inch of her home.

The screens in her room kept her abreast of what was happening below. The dreadnought's technology was spectacular compared to what they had on land. The screens sensed the direction of her face and followed her around the room as she dressed, always a glance away.

They continually switched views, showing her different parts of the world.

It was pure luck that she looked up when she did because three seconds later, the image changed.

"Go back," she told the AI.

"How far?"

"Last image."

It switched back to a single swath of black land that was surrounded by fire.

"Increase image tenfold," she directed the AI. She wasn't sure what she was looking at, but she wanted to see it better. Something was off in that spot.

The image grew larger on the screen, and suddenly she was looking at what appeared to be a gigante, a man of some sort, and a four-legged animal.

"Back up the image. Show me what happened to create this."

The image turned dark for a moment, then Cristin was watching a dogfight between two corvettes. One was hers, the other had come from the capital. She watched as her fighter easily disabled the other, and that was when something very strange happened.

The corvette crashed, but in a way that didn't destroy it. Instead, it slid across the ground for a half-kilometer or so before coming to rest in the midst of the flames.

Then a gigante removed a boulder that was burning like the rest of the area and stepped out. He began spraying some type of fire extinguishing spray, burning all the while. The nanotech exited his hands, healing him as he continued to spray the fire.

"Speed up."

The video's speed increased, and the gigante continued to fight the fire until only ash remained and the fire was at bay.

Finally, the man and animal hopped out of the dead corvette as if nothing had happened.

"Current state," the Ice Queen commanded.

The screen sped ahead until it reached the present time. The gigante was staring at the sky while the man appeared to be yelling at him, or at least speaking heatedly.

"Who are you?" she whispered. "Are you him? Are you the man who conquered a world and thought he could conquer my army with a tiny ship like that? What kind of beast are you?"

Louder, to the AI, she said, "Show me the capital."

The screen went black for a moment, then she was looking at a bird's-eye view of the city. The flames still had a hundred kilometers to go. There was plenty of time to get down there.

"Send a group of fifty warriors. Bring those three to me."

CHAPTER TWELVE

"Ah, spaceman, now you see. Look. You will not steal my glory yet." Nero extended his huge arm and hand into the sky, pointing.

Alistair had been in the middle of cursing the giant up and down, ignored by Nero. He finally shut his trap and turned to look in the air.

Ships were dropping from the dreadnought. It was too far away for Alistair to tell how many. He turned in a circle, looking at both the land and space to see where else they could come from.

He saw nothing.

"We've got to go right now. Can we get to your hole, Nero?"

"Spaceman, after everything that has happened to you, can you not trust just a little longer?" Nero asked without looking. "We cannot run from them. Even if you had begun to walk back or travel on a roc, *she* would still have seen you. Those up there would still be coming for you. I do not know how this ends, but I know we must go up high with them. There is no other way."

She.

The dispatched ships were entering the atmosphere, flames burning across their metal hulls and streaking back in long trails.

She.

Alistair forgot about the ships and looked at the giant's massive eyes as he followed their path. "Who is she, Nero? Who are you talking about?"

"The one you saw. I do not know her name, but I know she is a queen of the cold. Like you, she cares for only one thing. She is curious about you. That's who comes now. Running won't matter. Hiding won't matter. What the queen of cold wants, she will have, and right now she wants you."

Alistair let go of his defenses, his desire to return to their city, and his anger at the giant. "Obs, to me."

The drathe trotted over and sat. He and his master looked up at the ships, which were rapidly slowing their pace, the fire burning off the metal that encased whoever was inside. Alistair wore no armor. He had his Whip in a holster on his right side and a StarBeam on his left.

Are they right? The AllMother and the AllSeer? Is fate directing this, and we're just playing our parts? If so, he'd played his perfectly by training his mind these past few months.

He was going to see the shepherd, and he needed to let someone know he was still alive.

Alistair closed his eyes and sent two sentences toward the woman he hoped had some ability left.

I'm here. I'm still fighting.

The AllMother had not left her spot at the table. She wasn't sure she could walk right now without falling, and no one else needed to worry about her at this moment. She remained seated and watched what Thoreaux threw up on the holovid.

The AllMother's lesson with Alistair had weakened her, but that wasn't the reason her legs would fail if she stood.

She, perhaps more than anyone else at this table, believed in Prometheus. She had searched all but a few years of her life for this man. Every time he fell or faced insurmountable odds, she never wavered in her belief that he would overcome.

That was what he did. He overcame.

She had just watched him fly recklessly against a much more adept pilot, lose disastrously, and crash into a fiery field. She was weak from the loss, so that much that she couldn't feel his strength, his power, from a few hundred kilometers away?

The AllMother hadn't said those things to Thoreaux or Servia or the rest, but she thought Jeeves was right. The chance that he remained alive was small, probably smaller than the AI recognized.

She should be able to feel him, but she couldn't.

That meant that her life, her movement—they were over. There would be no search for a replacement. Nay, there would *be* no replacement. Thoreaux, the gods bless him, was not equipped for a battle like that, and he knew it.

Even Caesar, the mighty giant, would die long before reaching Earth.

If Prometheus was dead, they would all die in a few short hours.

Given that overwhelming knowledge, standing would be too much. She would wait until everyone had left or remain here all night. The AllMother wouldn't worry these people as they tried to salvage this disaster.

She couldn't cry. She could show no emotion.

She had to be the leader she'd always been.

Though it was over.

Thoreaux was back and forth across the room, taking messages from Jeeves, handing out orders through the AI, talking directly to Pro's council. He was handling it quite well. The anger in him had driven away the sadness, and he would do his best to save this world.

He will fail, the old woman thought. *I have failed him. His parents. Servia and her parents. I put too much faith in one man, and perhaps my brother was right. Perhaps his fate is the true one. His wind the one that will carry me back to Earth.*

All at once, the AllMother felt like dying.

The chair moved before the AllMother knew what was happening. One moment she was sitting at the round table, and the next, the chair was swiftly heading toward the wall. It was moving so fast, she didn't even have time to try to grip the floor with her shoes.

It hit the wall, her head nearly smacking into it too—which later she'd realize would have done as much damage to this endeavor as anything if she'd been knocked out.

The AllMother managed to stay conscious, then the

words fell on her like an unexpected wave. She grew cold and could focus on nothing but remembering to breathe.

She'd only seen such power once, and even then, it wasn't this skilled. The AllMother had seen it when Prometheus killed an army of gigantes that was about to kill him, throwing everyone and everything against the wall.

Now that pressure was focused. There was no denying who had sent it, and especially not the message.

I'm here. I'm still fighting.

Thoreaux turned from a screen on the other side of the room, the bang of the chair against the wall grabbing his attention. Servia had been staring at a DataTrack in her hand, facing the opposite way, and she quickly looked up too.

"What..." Thoreaux started to say, then stopped. He must have seen the AllMother's pale face, wide eyes, and open mouth. Perhaps he thought she was having a stroke.

Servia dropped the DataTrack and rushed across the room, Thoreaux only a moment behind her.

They went to their knees, all four hands reaching out to touch the closest thing to a mom either of them had.

"Are you okay?"

"What's wrong?"

"Do we need doctors?"

The questions ran over each other and were fired at her so quickly it would have been hard for anyone to answer them.

The AllMother didn't even hear them.

Her face still pale, her eyes still wide, she smiled. "Prometheus lives."

CHAPTER THIRTEEN

Ares had thought a lot since they'd left the black box. They were traveling in the fourth dimension now, moving at a much faster rate, and they'd been doing it for quite some time.

Wherever they were going, it was farther out than he thought anyone had ever gone.

Except that couldn't be true because someone had programmed this damned thing. Someone had been here before. Someone held the algorithm.

Ares's father Adrian hadn't spoken much about the gods when he was a boy, but there was a lot of time to think on this trip, and he found himself contemplating them.

He and Veena had kicked everything they could think of about the black box back and forth. He'd run out of ideas about what it could mean or what the real test had been. He thought Veena had too.

Things had changed between them. Nothing romantic —Ares didn't think that would *ever* interest either of them.

In the beginning, they'd been reluctant comrades. When they'd left together, they'd been reluctant partners because there was no one else.

The reluctance had faded. She'd come back to die at his side, and for Ares, there was no greater loyalty. He'd tried to fend off the robots and told her to run for her life while he died. He didn't know what that meant to her. Neither of them felt comfortable discussing those feelings with the other, which was fine.

It had meant something, though, and Ares could feel the difference in her.

They were both in the ship's little lounge. The vessel had a huge collection of media they could consume, everything from novels to endless holovid programs, some that went back before the Commonwealth. Ares had spent a good bit of time watching those, especially a little cartoon called *Rick and Morty*. It was a humorous program that dealt with space, time travel, multiverses, and a number of other things.

It was crazy what humans had thought up back then.

A thousand years in the future, Ares wished that space was as easy as the mad scientist had made it seem.

While watching that program, he began to consider the gods because the mad scientist Morty seemed as powerful as a god in his own hilariously goofy way.

"What are you watching?" he called over the back of his chair. His feet were up on a counter, and the program was casting in the air in front of him. He was thankful someone had gone back to the old shows, made them three-dimensional, and allowed them to be played on a holovid. Two-dimensional during this forever trip would drive a man to drink.

Only there wasn't anything to drink on this ship.

"Underground documentary on the first Ascendant. I would have never been able to see this on Earth. The man might have been a genius, but he was also a monster. I imagine whoever made this was killed off quick."

"Mind if I interrupt?" he asked.

"All this politeness, Ares? I'm not sure I can handle it."

"I'll take that as a yes." He didn't turn around but paused the program with a wave of his hand. "You ever think about the gods? Do you believe in them?"

"Don't you find that odd? Everyone in our Solar System knows about the gods. We know their names. Sure, some worship different gods and a few backward people are monotheistic, but we all know about some power greater than ours, yet people hardly discuss it. We are taught it as children, and that's it."

"I haven't thought about that before. I guess it's true, though. It's been like that as long as anyone knows."

Veena spun so that she was facing the back of his chair. "No. That's what some of this documentary is about. People used to attend huge cathedrals. They'd pray daily. There was even a sizable number of people who believed in no god. Now, it's like we all believe, but they don't matter to us."

Ares thought about that for a second, staring at the wild-haired scientist suspended in the air in front of him. "Do you believe in them?"

"Yeah, I suppose I do. I've got no reason to doubt them."

"Do you think they watch us? Do you think they're

watching this thing happening between the Commonwealth and Alistair?"

She shook her head. "Nah. If the gods cared, someone like the original Ascendant wouldn't have risen to power."

Ares turned so the two faced each other. "You don't think that was for the best?"

She let out a large sigh. "I don't know. That's the real question, isn't it? The wars ended. We have abundant energy that shows no sign of ever running out. All we have to do is bend the knee. I think about Kane and that sometimes."

"What do you mean?"

Veena slid down in her chair a bit and looked at the ceiling. "I mean, he served the Commonwealth for decades. No offense to present company, but he was probably the greatest Titan ever to live. He saw all the good the Commonwealth did, but in a single move, he pitted the entire empire against him." She glanced at Ares. "I'm not sure I've ever asked this, but do you know what he did?"

Ares nodded, a little smirk on his face. "He was sent after two Subversives. He was supposed to put them down, just like always." He shook his head, still smiling. "I almost can't believe it, sitting here thinking about it now. Just so ridiculous."

"What?"

Ares rolled his eyes. "They told him they had kids, and they didn't want their kids to grow up without parents or something similar. Alistair let them go."

"That's it? That's all he did? He let two Subversives go?"

Ares couldn't quit smirking as he nodded. "That's it. Two Subversives, and I was sent in to kill him. When I didn't do it, the Subversives took him in, and the Ascendant burned a planet."

Veena straightened. "How does that make any fucking sense, Ares? None of it does."

The smile dropped off his face. For the first time, he realized he hadn't thought any of it through and was embarrassed. "I... Gods, I just followed orders."

"We both did," Veena said as if she hardly heard him. Her mind was whirring. "First, why would the Subversives take in someone like him? He hunted them for decades, killed them like dogs in the street. Second, *why* would the Ascendant care so much? He was a great Titan, but he was only one man. So what that you didn't kill him. Was one man going to bring down a system?"

Ares was stunned into silence. She was right; none of it added up. The entire story was ridiculous.

"Look at this." Veena turned in her chair and waved her hand across the holovid. The image reversed until they were looking at an old photo taken from space. Ares had seen it before—the nuclear blast sites that had killed so many people. "That's a lot of unlivable space," she continued. "The story goes that after that nuclear war, the first Ascendant decided he couldn't let mankind kill itself, and that's what started his conquest. Now look at this, a thousand years later."

She pulled up a current space view. The unlivable spots were down to two. Veena leaned back in her chair. "A thousand years later, why are there two spots on Earth that you can't go to?"

"Radiation half-life," Ares said, though his voice sounded weak to his ears.

"Yeah, that's the story, but what else could it be, Ares? Think."

He was at a loss. He had no clue.

"It makes sense." Veena was almost speaking to herself. "If the Ascendant was creating this epic artificial intelligence, something he could upload himself to, something that could practically see into the future, they would need server space. A lot of server space, especially a thousand years ago. As time progresses, the story is the radiation half-life allowed people to move back in, but technology is continuously improving. Maybe they didn't need the server space anymore."

"Yeah," Ares said, finally catching up. "But technology improves faster than that. From all those radiation areas down to two in a thousand years? They wouldn't need nearly that much server space."

"True, if the AI didn't improve, which it had to. The original was probably incompatible with the current state of technology, so *more* server space might be needed to power it."

Ares opened his mouth, but the words caught in his throat.

It made sense.

Veena wasn't done. "If all that is true, the only rational explanation is that the AI made a decision about Kane. It decided burning a planet was worth the chance of killing him. Why?"

Ares' eyes opened wide. "It knows. It knows he might be able to bring down the Commonwealth."

"We're making a lot of logical leaps, I'll grant that, but what makes more sense? One Titan lets two people go, the ones he hunted for years take him in and make him a leader, and the Ascendant decides he's worth chasing across the universe? Or, the algorithm exists because the AI exists, and it knows more than any of us do."

She spun her chair slowly.

"I can hardly say it aloud," she told him.

"It knows he has a chance to bring down the Commonwealth," Ares whispered, hardly able to believe it but not able to disprove it.

The AI spoke from above, breaking into their thoughts. "I am dropping us into the third dimension. At planned speed, we will reach the algorithm in just under two hours."

The two of them shot up. Veena was already moving toward the bridge, taking control like the Primus she used to be. "Why are you just telling me this?" she asked the AI.

"It's the requirement of the digits you gave me," it answered. "I did not know until milliseconds before I told you. Dropping into the third dimension now."

Veena felt the difference immediately, a huge relief to her entire body. The intensity of upper dimensions took its toll.

She reached the bridge moments later, feeling like she could already breathe better.

"Show me where we're going," she demanded.

Screens lit up as she sat in her chair. She saw an orb in front of her, and at first glance, it looked naturally made, not like the box.

"Give me all the information we have on it. Is it a planet that formed naturally?"

"There is no information on this planet," it responded.

"There has been no known contact with it, but from early scans, it appears to be formed of organic materials."

"Weapons?"

"Initial scans show it is well-fortified. Space defense system. Land-to-air missiles available."

Veena didn't know what to think. She had believed they'd have time to figure out where they were going, though now she realized that had been foolish. Whoever had started this game didn't want them to know anything. "Is it possible to turn around?"

"I cannot until we have landed."

Veena pulled the ship's controls to her and started trying to change course. Nothing reacted as she touched panels and changed coordinates. For the second time, she'd lost control of her ship.

"Well," she said as she leaned back in her chair, "we're going to land. No doubt about that."

Ares was standing next to her seat, looking at the screens. "AI, can you predict where we're going to land?"

"Not with any real accuracy. If my computations are right, we will be five or ten kilometers outside a populated zone. There's movement on the planet, though the screens can't show it this far out."

"What is going on?" Veena wondered aloud. "Where is the nearest populated star system?"

"One hundred million light-years."

A planet no one had contact with that had no outside commerce, somehow existing this far out? A *populated* planet.

"Keep giving me data as it comes in, and feed your voice through the whole ship," she told the AI, then looked at

Ares. "We'll know everything together. You want to see how well those hoverblades work?"

His face was solemn as he nodded.

They'd come all this way. Neither of them was prepared.

They both knew it, too.

All of the philosophizing and theorizing left Ares' head. He didn't want to bring the battle to this planet. That wasn't why he'd come. However, he didn't see any other way. It was clear that whoever had created this little puzzle meant to try to kill them and had killed a lot of others in the process. The black box's AI had told them only one group had ever returned, and it had returned without the algorithm.

Ares spent the next two hours preparing the hoverblades. If the ship was landing them ten kilometers out, they were most likely going to need ground transportation. The blades would take care of that.

Truthfully, neither of them knew what to expect. Their AI had given them information for the next thirty minutes. The planet was populated by humans or some other race, but it couldn't tell which. There were many populated land areas across the planet, but the oddest—and last thing—it gave them was that there appeared to be no water or plant life. It was a dry, barren world.

Then the AI's scans had stopped. No technical issues, no other problems—it just stopped being able to scan the planet. Veena's screens had stopped working, too. Either this planet had technology that stopped outside viewers from seeing it, or someone knew they were coming and wanted them blind.

Either way, the tech matched what they'd seen in that black box, far more advanced than anything Ares or Veena was familiar with.

The ship touched down easily, and like last time, the AI died. Ares and Veena stood in the cargo bay next to their hoverblades, though neither was eager to step outside.

They both heard the sounds. They were either motors or the most ferocious growls Ares had ever heard. Someone—or something—was waiting for them, so it didn't look like they would need the hoverblades.

"You think we can wait 'em out? Just stay inside, and maybe they'll leave?" Ares joked without looking at Veena.

She didn't have a witty response. "One way or another, I think whoever is out there is going to get to us. I'd rather do it in a way that doesn't destroy our ship. Are you ready?"

Ares stood in his MechSuit, Whip in hand. "Ready."

Veena raised her hand and passed it over the wall panel.

The cargo bay's door slowly lowered until it touched the ground.

Ares' HUD immediately did an air scan. "Oxygen's fine," he said, but he'd moved on in his mind. His eyes blinked as he tried to figure out what he was looking at. It was so odd, so inhuman, that he couldn't process it.

The noise they'd heard hadn't been a motor but a thousand small flying robots. The only thing Ares' mind could compare them to was heads, though they weren't shaped like that. Each of the robots was round and had a ring of red lights around its middle and five jelly-like tentacles branching off one side.

"What in hades?" Veena whispered.

The tentacles appeared to be made of organic matter, while the body looked robotic.

They were whipping around in a huge circle that nearly touched the ground and stretched twenty meters high. Around and around they went, the air churning so quickly that it had made a sound like a motor.

Ares took a step forward.

The robots stopped. Red lights stared at the two humans, tentacles waving in the windless air.

"We mean you no harm," Veena said softly.

The robots then did something even stranger. While some remained still, others started flying forward, then stopping just in front of the one that had flown before them. Ares saw fairly quickly what they were doing.

"They're building a bridge to us," he said through his helmet.

"Are we supposed to climb onto it?"

"I think so," he answered.

The bridge touched down where the cargo bay door connected to the ship.

"Come." The voice emanated from all the robots. It sounded like what it was, robots trying to speak a human language.

Ares could kill some of them, he knew, but not all. They could rush him, and there were enough to do serious damage. They could also just fly away. They couldn't retreat into the ship; that was obvious.

They'd come here to get the algorithm, so forward was the only way.

Veena didn't give him much choice, though. She moved toward the door.

Ares followed, and they stepped onto the robot bridge at almost the same time. The robots started to swirl, and the construction lifted into the air.

After they rose above the ship and started forward, Ares only needed one glance to know where they were heading.

A city full of machines.

CHAPTER FOURTEEN

The dispatched ships had just breached the atmosphere, this time heading into space. The whole endeavor had taken maybe a half-hour, and Alistair was wondering if he'd made the right decision.

The giant sitting next to him would say yes, he knew. Obs, immobile at Alistair's feet, might differ.

There wasn't any going back, though.

The dispatch had landed. Five ships.

Alistair had never seen anything like the creatures that had stepped off. They were bred in a lab, though hugely different from gigantes. Their facial features were man-like, their eye colors the same, a crystal-blue. All fifty of the men had pure white hair that resembled a human's, long and pulled back in a ponytail.

Once you moved past their necks, things stopped making sense. They were covered in thick white hair, though nothing like the strands on their head. This was animal fur, a pelt.

They had all looked at Alistair and his crew with something akin to disgust. One or two had spit on the ground, and Alistair had nearly drawn his Whip.

Nero had stayed him, though. He'd placed a huge hand on his shoulder and simply said, "We go up."

Now Alistair was separated from his Whip and immobile as well. He hadn't seen the technology they used before, though it was easy to understand. Two straight bands had been slapped on the gigante and Alistair, one on their wrists, one on their ankles.

After that, the only things he was able to move were his jaw, tongue, and eyes. Everything else was frozen.

Obs had nearly ripped into one of the human-animal hybrids and only calmed down after Alistair convinced the creatures to let him place the bands on Obs' legs.

Two of the hybrids stood in the prisoner bay with Alistair's group. They'd said nothing the whole time, not even while slapping the bands on. For all Alistair knew, they couldn't speak.

They'd stared at Nero as if they knew he was also a bred species.

"Have you ever seen anything like them?" Alistair asked, his first time speaking since boarding the ship.

"No," Nero answered. "This is my first time in space, remember? You were the first outside visitor to my planet."

The gigante didn't seem concerned about anything that was happening. His damned dream had done some work on his mental state.

The ship finally docked with the dreadnought. Three floating slabs were brought in, and the hybrids lifted all three and dropped them on the apparent transportation. Alistair wasn't just impressed with the hybrids' strength, he was shocked by it. One alone lifted Nero as if he'd been little more than a pillow.

Gigantes were different from humans, but they were human-based.

These things were new.

"It's okay, Obs," Alistair said as the slabs started to move without direction. He imagined the animal was in a state of near-panic, if not outright terror.

Alistair could only look at the ceiling as the three slabs wound through corridors. He saw two of the hybrids walking with them out of the corner of his eye, though they paid him no mind. Alistair was trying to keep track of time because he needed to know how close the army was to the capital. By the time they reached the room, he thought about forty minutes had passed.

He might have one hour, maybe two.

As they reached the room, the slabs moved to the far wall, then stood up. None of the three slid down, though, since some force from the slabs kept them pinned against them.

"Nero, you still with me?" Alistair asked.

"I do not like space as much as I thought I would," he said in his stilted manner. He sounded disappointed and grumpy as if they had not enjoyed their accommodations on vacation rather than being held captive.

"Sorry to hear that, Nero. Really, sorry." Alistair would have smacked the giant if his hands had been capable of moving. "Next time, I recommend not taking an enemy ship. You might find things a bit more to your liking."

He heard the giant chuckle from his right side. "I like you, spaceman. You make me laugh."

The hybrid beasts left the room and they were alone. Alistair understood that mattered little; everything in this room was being watched by some ever-present AI, and it would only take a word for their blood to spill all over the floor.

Alistair estimated another ten minutes passed before the woman Nero had called the queen of cold entered.

She stopped at the door, and Alistair took her in. When he'd seen her in his mind, things had been hazy and tinted with odd colors.

Now he saw clearly.

She was tall for an Earthborn woman, though that meant nothing in this part of space. She was very thin, and her hair was the same white as the hybrids, long and tied back the same way. She had a certain hardness, one that radiated from the set of her jaw and the way she held herself.

This is a true warlord, Alistair thought. She wasn't like the outlaws or the businessmen he'd encountered. This was someone who had never known comfort and who conquered because that was all she knew.

"Are you the one who took this planet?" she asked, her voice as cold as the rest of her.

"I'm the one who freed the slaves," he answered.

"I would like to speak to you for a bit before our war starts. I won't offer any lies or false hope. You will never make it off this ship. You will die here. However, if you're willing to speak to me, I'll make it an easy death."

She stared at him, her hands at her sides, no fear and nothing to hide.

"Here? Like this?" he asked.

"No. I'll let you walk with me. I have much to do, and I need to work while we talk."

"I'll speak to you as long as you let my friends come with me."

She shrugged. "That doesn't matter. You all must know that if one of you makes a move to hurt me or anyone in this ship, you'll die immediately." Her eyes fell on Nero. "Gigante, do you understand that?"

"I do."

She looked at Obs next. "A drathe? I saw one when I was young but haven't since. It understands what I'm saying, right? If it tries to attack me, it will die immediately." Her eyes found Alistair again. "You can control it?"

"He'll obey me."

She took in a deep breath and nodded, then walked across the floor and touched Alistair's ankle bracelet. It straightened and fell to the floor. He immediately felt his body sag; the slabs were attached to the bracelets somehow. She touched the one on his wrists next, and he dropped to the floor.

Alistair let himself squat, stretching his muscles while she removed the restraints from Nero and Obs.

The drathe hit the ground awkwardly, bounced up, and trotted to where Alistair was squatting.

Nero stood, rubbing his wrists.

"My name is Cristin," the woman said from the last slab. "I'm known as the Ice Queen, though that moniker comes more from my home than anything sinister."

I doubt that, Alistair thought but didn't say.

She pointed at the door. "The drathe and the gigante will walk in front of us. As we walk, you'll see a blue line

179

on the floor. Just follow that, and we'll get to where I need to be."

Nero was quiet, though he patted his leg for Obs to come. The drathe looked up at Alistair, and he gave a small nod.

Nero started to walk, and Obs followed. The Ice Queen stepped over to Alistair, who stood up. "Let's go. There's much to be done, and if the people I came here with knew I was wasting time speaking to you, I'd get an earful about it."

There wasn't any fear or deference in the woman when she spoke of the other warlords, only a slight sense of annoyance.

The group exited the room, and Alistair saw the blue line. Nero and Obs walked five meters in front of them, with the drathe glancing over his shoulder every thirty seconds.

"How close are you to the capital?" Alistair asked.

"Distance or time?"

"Time."

"We should be there within an hour."

Alistair's timeline had been right, and he now knew how long he had to do *something*. He just didn't know what. His position could be worse, though. She wanted to talk, and in doing so, he'd learn about her too. He hadn't had the chance to know his enemy before, not truly. "Why do you want to talk to me? If you're going to kill me and everyone I know, what does it matter what I have to say?"

They turned right into another hall. The pace was an easy one, which showed how confident she felt.

"I've never met a man like you," she said. "At least, I

don't think I have, though you might prove me wrong. I'm curious about why you conquered that planet, only to turn around and free its most valuable resource."

"You don't understand why someone would want to free slaves?"

She shook her head but didn't look at him. "If there's one truth in the universe, it's that it doesn't care about us. Stars explode and consume entire civilizations. Meteors wreck planets with abandon. They don't care who they kill. I'd venture to say the universe is malevolent. It may be trying to kill us."

Another turn and the blue line ended. She stopped. "Go through the door on your right."

Nero and Obs did as they were told, and Cristin started walking again.

"Nature," she continued, "seems to have followed the universe's lead. Every creature must consume to live. They kill each other, and then we evolved, and we kill each other. So no, it doesn't make much sense that someone would risk their lives for people that aren't family, especially if they don't plan to profit off them."

They turned into the room as she finished speaking. They'd reached the bridge, a massive one, full of movement. Alistair's mind quickly counted the number of people—a hundred. It was the largest bridge he'd ever seen, and he couldn't imagine what all these people were doing.

The Ice Queen walked over to the leader's chair. It was raised above the floor. She sat and pointed to the wall. "Gigante and drathe, you stand over there, and remember my warning."

Nero's eyes were wide, shock and wonder on his face as

he took in the bridge. "This is marvelous," he said as he meandered to the wall she'd pointed at. Obs sniffed the deck, his eyes following people suspiciously. After a moment, he followed the giant.

Alistair remained standing next to the woman's chair, staring at the movement in front of him. Large screens showed the world's destruction, with the middle one focused on the capital. No soldiers or ships had breached it yet, but he could see how close they were. The fires weren't far off.

Cristin pulled up a holovid-like control screen in front of her and began typing on it as she spoke. "So, why'd you do it?"

"It was the right thing to do." Alistair didn't know what answer she wanted. To him, it was self-evident.

"It was stupid, perhaps the dumbest thing you could do. Did you have any plan after you freed them?"

"I'm not sure I did, and I guess that means I didn't. I'd hoped some of them would join me, but they all ended up wanting to be my slaves."

She paused what she was doing and turned to look at him. "That's the way of the universe. The weak bow to the strong. You refused them?"

Alistair felt like he might lose his mind. He was standing here discussing the past while Thoreaux was about to lose his life. His voice remained calm, though. "In a way. We were in the process of teaching them when you all decided to show up."

The Ice Queen shook her head in disbelief and turned back to her panel. "You would teach them to be free and hope they followed you. It makes no sense. You see that, don't you?"

Alistair said nothing.

"What was your end goal when you freed these slaves and taught them to love you?"

His eyes narrowed, and he gazed at her. "Why does it matter?"

"You're a very different man. I'd like to know you some. We've been over this. Now, what's your end goal? Would you have come to my planet and tried to free my Lukos?"

"Are those the hybrid creatures that brought us here?"

"Yes," Cristin said. "They're bred like the gigantes, only a much better product. You've opened the door for me to expand that business, and for that, I'm grateful. Were you coming to my planet next?"

Alistair chuckled. "I didn't even know you existed. Had I known, no, I wouldn't have come. I went to the gigantes because I met one, and he's one of the noblest creatures I've ever encountered. If I could free a species like him, I had to do it."

"Ah." The Ice Queen nodded. "Is it the gigante against the wall?"

"No. He's in the city you're about to destroy."

"But you consider him family? This noble giant?"

Alistair opened his mouth, then paused. When this began, he'd joined a group he despised because it was the only way to get back to Luna. Then he'd decided to lead them because their goal made sense. Then he risked his life for his second in command because...

Because I love him like a brother.

Yet, he'd never thought of those people as family. He'd

freed an entire planet because he'd started to love one of their kind.

Now he knew the truth.

"Yes, he's my brother."

Cristin moved the holovid screen with a flick of her wrist, and another one popped up in its place. "That I understand. It leads me to another question, though. First, what is your name?"

"Alistair Kane."

"Alistair," the Ice Queen continued as if she were discussing a recipe, "what have you done to your brother? You've sacrificed him, as well as the rest of your family down there. You're a perfect specimen of humanity, if modified. You could have done anything you wanted, yet you chose a path that will leave your family dead. Do you think you were the right one to lead them, given what's about to happen?"

Alistair's jaw twitched. He'd dealt with his guilt about his decisions, but to hear this bitch talk about it…

In his mind, Alistair felt Prometheus bang on the door, wanting to be let out of the room he was kept in.

His voice changed as he spoke, unable to keep emotion out of it. "No one else in this universe could do what I did. You talk about them monopolizing a market when your product is better, but you did nothing. You sat on whatever planet you're from and watched as stronger people took from you. Was I the right one to lead? I'm the only one to lead them."

The Ice Queen stopped what she was doing and turned her gaze on him. It was as cold as whatever planet she came from. She was quiet as she stared, but Alistair did not look away. Whatever hardships this warlord had endured, whatever strength lay in her, Alistair didn't care.

She eventually looked away. There was silence for a minute or two, painful minutes because Alistair understood they only had about thirty until the battle began.

When Cristin next spoke, her voice was hard and her hands rapidly flipped through commands on the panel. "I understand family. That's why I'm here. I will kill your family if it means mine will be better off. Perhaps you're right, Alistair Kane; you were the one to lead them. That's the difference between us, though. Your heart is too kind, and mine is cold to everything but family. My family will thrive while yours dies."

Alistair glanced to his right, looking at Obs against the wall. The drathe was staring at him and had heard everything they'd said.

When Alistair thought back to that moment, he could never be sure if he saw what he thought he had, and Obs wasn't capable of speaking.

Yet at that moment, he thought he saw Obs nod.

The drathe was giving him permission.

The banging on the door inside his head stopped because Alistair opened it and Prometheus stepped out.

CHAPTER FIFTEEN

To say that Thoreaux was out of his element would be like saying a fish flying through the air was in the wrong place.

He'd watched his leader, his best friend, do perhaps the dumbest thing the man had ever done.

Then he'd watched the man die.

Then he'd scrambled to try to defend a city that would surely burn.

As if that wasn't enough, his spiritual leader had been thrown against a wall, apparently by his dead best friend, who wasn't dead.

There hadn't been time to consider what that meant. Hearing the AllMother's message, *I'm here. I'm still fighting,* had been more than enough to get Thoreaux moving.

Yet, life hadn't thrown enough at the Plutonian. He then watched ships take his best friend to a dreadnought that was on its way to kill them all.

The ships were close, hovering just outside the city's walls and slowly moving over the buildings. They remained outside the atmosphere, so there wasn't any way to attack them. Thoreaux could only watch as they came closer.

Now, as he stared at the holovid that showed the enemy coming closer, it looked as if they'd stopped moving.

Jeeves spoke from the ceiling's speakers. "I can confirm the dreadnoughts have stopped moving. Most of the other fleet has stopped moving or is slowing."

Thoreaux, surrounded by Pro's council, leaned on the table, staring at the holovid. "Does anyone know what is happening? Does anyone have a clue?"

No one answered since they were as lost as he was.

"Jeeves, they can attack from where they are, right?" Thoreaux asked.

"Yes, though their death toll will increase by about twenty percent," the AI responded. "There's no logical reason for them not to hang directly over the city."

Caesar had been standing to the side, but when the AI finished speaking, he started moving toward the door.

Thoreaux snapped his attention to the giant. "Where are you going?"

Caesar stopped but didn't turn around, just looked over his shoulder. "To battle. Alistair is up there fighting for us right now. I'm going to fight for him here."

The giant left the room.

Thoreaux looked at Servia. His sister-in-arms had one eyebrow raised and a devilish smirk on her lips. "He's right. It's the only thing that makes any sense. That dumb bastard is up there doing something. We've all been wanting him to do something this whole time, and now he finally is."

Thoreaux turned to his lover Faitrin next. She was

leaning back in her chair. "You remember how scared I was for the enemy a few months ago if Pro turned you loose?"

He nodded.

"I think you need to put me in a corvette and follow that giant outside. I'm not scared for them anymore. Bring me back some scalps, love."

Thoreaux straightened up.

Relm stood on the other side of the table. "Your woman's a savage, broth, but right now, I think we all have to turn into savages. I'll be damned if that giant is the only one who gets any glory in this."

He started walking toward the door. The bastard already had a MechPulse strapped to his back.

"Jeeves," Thoreaux said, "get a corvette over here and put the pilot in it. Servia, you try to keep us organized. My woman wants scalps, and I don't mean to disappoint her."

Just like that, the attitude shifted. Thoreaux would follow Prometheus to fight the gods if that was what the man demanded.

Right now, he just wanted to fight some warlords, and after all he'd given this group, what were a few more dead bodies?

Relm was outside the room and walking down the hall when they heard his shout.

"*Ave*, Prometheus!"

Alistair was a reckless man. He rushed into things without forethought, and that was perhaps his greatest fault. He relied on his physical and mental abilities to get him out of every situation, trusting them as if they would never falter.

They had faltered, though, when he was shot out of the sky a few hours before.

Yet, his greatness was somehow tied to the recklessness. He could never have achieved any of what he'd done had he not trusted himself.

A double-edged sword, but one that seemed to cut the enemy worse than him.

Cristin de Monaham had thought she could come to know this man in a brief conversation or at least know him better. As he'd described his reasoning to her, she came to think him a fool—someone who had sacrificed his family for a higher good that didn't exist.

The Ice Queen thought she understood the man.

Until the moment she was thrust out of her chair without anyone touching her and tossed across her bridge above her pilots to slam into the opposite wall.

Then she realized she understood little about this human.

Slightly before she was tossed, Alistair grew reckless again and leaned into his superhuman abilities.

———

Prometheus had looked to the left and simply willed it.

The woman who was known as the Ice Queen rose into the air and was thrown with as much force as his mind could muster.

The hybrids seemed to appear from nowhere, twenty of them. Some stared at their queen as she sped through the air while the rest went to kill the only man who was close to her.

They got within three meters, then once again, Prometheus simply willed it.

They flew backward, bending the metal walls when they slammed into them.

Obs grabbed one out of the air by his foot, tossing the creature to the ground before diving at his throat.

Nero stepped away from the wall and looked at Prometheus. "Most of that was in the dream."

Prometheus could feel his Whip. The connection between the two of them couldn't be broken; it was built into the weapon. He needed it, and he had to rely on that wind the AllMother had talked about to make that happen.

"Obs," he snapped. "To me!"

The animal looked up, blood on his maw. He bounded to his master in two easy leaps.

Pro squatted so he was at eye level with the beast. "My Whip. If we're gonna live, I have to have it. Can you find it?"

The animal's eyes narrowed, containing a freakish wisdom compared to the blood and guts covering his fur.

A moment passed, and the beast fled from the room.

Obstinate, known to his loved ones as "Obs," had waited his entire life to find the person he would soul-bond with. Measuring the animal's intelligence was impossible due to the nature of his mind. Many across the galaxy doubted the soul-bond, calling it a myth.

That had never mattered to Obs, who hadn't even had a name until meeting his soul-bond. The bond was hard for any human to understand, so as the animal rushes from the room to do his master's bidding, it might be valuable to take a few moments to describe its effects.

When he was a pup, it was an ache. No one had to tell him what he searched for; he innately understood it, the same as he had to drink milk from his mother after he was born. As he grew older, the ache changed, probably because pain like that couldn't be dealt with for too long. It changed into a trusting search. As a gift from whatever gods had made them, the drathe were meant to meet one master. It was, as the AllSeer might say, their fate. Obs had trusted that one day he would meet the person he was meant for, but he'd also kept a keen eye out for him.

The animal hadn't understood how powerful the bond would be, and he didn't want to accidentally miss the human if they came near him.

The drathe dreamed of his master in a way Alistair would have found eerily similar to his own dreams. He saw his face, his red eyes, his perfect form. Years before he met Alistair, the drathe saw him when he slept.

When the shaman gave Obs to Linc, transferring him across trillions of light-years, Obs had known he was heading in the right direction. He could feel it. Linc, the new keeper, wasn't his soul-bond, but he was bringing the animal closer.

While Alistair was being flown through multiple dimensions, heading from Earth to Pluto, giddy panic had set in. He couldn't tell anyone. He didn't have the words to describe it, the ones he naturally understood from others, yet he felt the bond growing *physically* closer.

His fate was nearly upon him.

When Alistair landed on Pluto, Obs lost the ability to sleep. He could hardly even lie down. He paced incessantly, driving Linc mad. He couldn't help it, though.

The moment he saw Alistair Kane was burned in the animal's mind. He'd sat outside the small room, staring in, frightened in the best way. The animal wasn't capable of understanding what was going through the human's mind at that time, that some huge dog-like creature was about to be thrust on him.

Had Obs been able to consider it from Alistair's point of view, he wouldn't have cared.

Obs had found his home, and it was wherever this man was.

Now they were tied together in a way others couldn't understand. Obs knew that if Prometheus died, he would too. That was the way of the drathe, yet his death wasn't what motivated the animal. He would fight an entire army to keep his soul-bond alive, even if it meant his death.

It was a loyalty humans could only understand when they thought about a mother and her children.

So when his master said find the Whip or we die, Obs didn't hear the "we" part. He heard, find the Whip or *I* die.

His master would die.

No force in the universe could have kept the animal from doing his master's bidding. He would find the Whip, or he would die.

There are an endless number of great things about animals, but the one humanity often overlooks is how much they trust their instincts. Obs didn't fret or worry about how he'd find the Whip, and when he *felt* the weapon, he didn't question that either. He could feel it because his soul-bond could feel it. Perhaps that was the difference between his and Alistair's ability to find the Whip. Men had a hard time being and trusting themselves. Thoughts and questions constantly plagued their minds.

Obs had no such issues.

The drathe flew through the halls, hundreds of pounds of muscle moving so quickly one could entirely miss him. He rounded corners and sped through corridor after corridor, trusting his instincts.

He slowed when he reached the door that held his master's murderous lasers.

For the first time, he heard the siren. The drathe had no idea how long it'd been going off, but he understood its meaning. Help was needed.

He crept up to the door, lowering himself almost to the ground, his muscles primed.

The door opened, and one of those strange-smelling manlike animals stood on the other side. It never had a chance.

Obs pounced, over two hundred pounds crashing into the unsuspecting creature. The drathe wasted no time; he ripped the thing's throat out and leaped on the second one.

The second hybrid was more prepared than the first, slugging Obs and trying to spin at the same time.

Obs took the punch in his ribs and flew against the wall. He didn't slow but found his feet and faced the enemy.

The hybrid's weapon sat on a table next to the Whip they'd probably been trying to figure out how to turn on.

He slowly started moving toward it. Obs understood that he had one chance to win this, and if the hybrid got the weapon, his master was going to die.

A cold focus came over the animal. No siren blared. Nothing in the universe existed but the slowly walking man.

The glance was Obs' opening. The hybrid looked at the table for a split-second.

The drathe launched himself with no thought for the consequences, like his master. The need to kill dominated.

The hybrid was inhumanly fast, faster even than the drathe.

He grabbed Obs under his front legs, but the animal's weight slammed them both against the wall. Snarls and spit flew from Obs' mouth as he bit and tore everything in front of him.

Blows rained on his ribs, but he didn't feel them.

In the end, Obs stood over the hybrid's body, gasping. His blood and that of the hybrid coated his fur.

He looked once more at the hybrid in a rare selfish act and yanked on the cadaver's neck, severing the spine.

A second wasted, but Obs couldn't help himself.

That small victory complete, he bounded to the table, put his front paws on it, and delicately reached down with his teeth.

He picked up his master's Whip, then once again bounded through the halls.

Alistair would have cared that he had perhaps sent his animal to his death.

Prometheus had no such concern. The beast would return, and Pro would destroy this place.

Nero's calm demeanor had been replaced by a rage Pro had never seen in a gigante. The hybrids that came for him were thrown across the bridge, breaking equipment and knocking out pilots.

Prometheus moved across the area like the wind. His mind was free, and while he didn't have his Whip, his hands and feet were deadlier than most men's weapons. Pilot or hybrid, Pro didn't care. He broke them all, anything that came toward him. Legs, knees, and skulls shattered beneath his speed and strength.

A siren was blaring, most likely throughout the ship. That meant more would come—many more.

He understood that they couldn't hold them off forever. He had to find the Ice Queen and put her down. He had to kill the shepherd, but he'd lost her in the battle.

Pro felt the wind of something coming at him and he turned, his mind slinging a monitor through the air to brain the attacker.

He found his hand buried in fur and a giant drathe hanging in mid-air, staring at him.

The monitor stopped centimeters from Obs' skull.

The animal held the Whip in his mouth.

"Good dog," Pro said, releasing the drathe and grabbing the Whip from his mouth as he fell. Obs hit the deck and lightly nipped his calf for the remark.

Prometheus' Whip unfurled, all three lasers sensing their owner's desire for destruction.

Hybrids as well as humans were flooding into the room. The Ice Queen's slaves and soldiers had come to save her.

A certain dead businessman would have recognized the god of death as he sprang at them. Prometheus cut through them, spinning, leaping, ducking... Bodies fell around him as if he were scything grain in a field.

More came, though. Prometheus didn't know where Nero or Obs or the Ice Queen were. He cut through the hordes, their screams and cries drowning out the blaring siren.

As he spun around one hybrid, decapitating him and plunging his Whip into the human running at him, he glanced at the queen's chair.

She stood just in front of it, smiling.

The siren quit blaring, and two voices replaced the noise.

The Ice Queen's and one Pro didn't recognize.

The battle halted as all turned toward the chair. The bitch was smiling at him. The male voice came over the speakers.

"You're godsdamn out of your mind, Cristin. Are we ready to launch the attack?"

The woman looked at Pro, still smiling. Her voice rang out over everyone. "Drop everything you have on the capital. Now."

"Dropping now," came the male's response, then his line clicked off.

The Ice Queen spoke once more and her voice was heard by everyone, but she was only speaking to one man on the bridge. "See you on the battlefield."

She sat on the chair, and it sank beneath the floor. The Ice Queen was gone.

Pro leaped over a table and cut down a pilot as he reached the spot where she'd been. A metal barrier had replaced the chair, cutting him off from her escape.

Obs bounded over to him.

Nero was standing at the edge of the bridge.

The flood of enemies had ceased. Those remaining were rushing out as their queen had commanded. Only the sounds of the dying filled the room.

The battle was no longer here.

It was in the capital.

So was the shepherd.

CHAPTER SIXTEEN

Servia had been in battles. She'd watched her lover die. She'd seen a planet burn, barely escaping with her life.

Yet, standing in what had once been a boardroom and was now a war room, she'd never witnessed anything like what she now saw.

It would have been beautiful if it wasn't so terrifying.

How is mankind so wonderful but so brutal? she wondered as she stepped to the window.

Red, yellow, and orange streaked through the sky. Some bands were wide, a half-kilometer. Others were much thinner, twice the height of a person.

The colors were beautiful, and the technology used to create them was genius. The result? Blood was about to spill across the land.

Servia had mapped out a projected plan of how they would attack, but Pro must have changed something in that dreadnought. They hadn't thought individuals would fall, raining from the sky like tiny bullets, but that was what she now saw.

Thousands of warriors in man-sized capsules shot from the dreadnoughts, aiming for the city.

Corvettes were breaching the planet's atmosphere, and soon their lasers and plasma blasters would devastate the people and buildings. Servia saw the massive delivery ships dropping as well; those were the ones creating huge streaks of color behind them. When they landed, thousands more soldiers would fill the city.

Would they return to the sky to get more? Or had Prometheus made that an impossibility?

"Jeeves," Servia said, "connect me to Thoreaux."

She heard a soft click in her ear, alerting her that she was on with him. "You seeing this?"

"It'd be impossible to miss." She heard the awe in his voice.

"Where are you?"

"Taking the north side. Caesar has the east. We've each got three squads of gigantes with us."

A quick moment of silence passed between the two.

"It's not gonna be enough, Serv," Thoreaux stated.

"Just keep fighting. I'm going to see what's going on with Faitrin. Out."

Jeeves, hearing the conversation, connected Servia to the pilot. "Faitrin, it's Servia. We've got thirty seconds until the individual soldiers are going to be within range. Are you in a place to kill some before they land?"

It was Jeeves' voice that came back since Faitrin had harmonized with her ship and was no longer speaking verbally. "Already in place. Lasers targeting the first one that breaches. We've got ten other corvettes out here now, too. I'm in contact with all. We'll deliver the best air defense we can."

"Good woman," Servia said and ended the connection.

She then took a brief few seconds, and for the first time in her life, prayed to the gods.

She prayed for two things: that they might somehow intervene to save the ones she loved, and if not that, she prayed for a quick and merciful defeat.

Prometheus stood among the dead. He'd killed a lot of them, probably half. He was staring at the remaining undamaged panels, watching as three armies first flew through space, then gravity pulled them toward the planet.

He had to figure out the best way to fight. He had a dreadnought now but no crew to run it, and it wasn't like he could open up the plasma sprayers on the city. He'd kill as many of his men as theirs.

Nero was pacing, glancing at the panels every few feet. The rage that had possessed him hadn't dissipated. The gigante's bloodlust was running high, and remaining here was aggravating it.

Prometheus saw only one way out. "We've got to find a smaller ship and get down there."

Nero grunted but said nothing as he continued walking to and fro.

Something clicked in Pro's mind. He hadn't thought about it before, and he wasn't even sure it would work. There were different trigger words for AIs, and the advanced ones like Jeeves could often tell by inflection or the question when they were being targeted with questions. Based on what he'd seen so far, he imagined the dreadnought's AI was more like the latter.

He just didn't know if his voice would be able to trigger it.

Pro turned his head up, another way that would allow the AI to know it was being queried. "Are there any available corvettes or two-man ships?" Obs was coming along, but they didn't want a ship that would require three pairs of hands.

"Yes," the AI said from the speakers. One of the panels the Ice Queen had used rose in front of Prometheus. A map of the ship was in front of it, with a red line leading from the bridge to where the ship was housed. "There are ten ships of that caliber still available. Would you like me to ready one for you?"

"Yes." Pro thought about one other thing. "Do we have any comms that can keep me connected to you during the flight and when I'm on land?"

"Affirmative." The AI wasn't programmed to sound human, though he imagined that had been done on purpose after meeting the bitch who owned it. "I will ensure that it is in the ship waiting for you."

"Time to go," Pro said.

Nero finally stopped pacing, grunted again, and walked toward the bridge's exit. Prometheus had memorized the map and started jogging.

Nero and Obs matched his pace easily, keeping a few feet behind him as he led the way.

They made it to the hangar bay in five minutes.

Prometheus had stepped back into his room for the time being, letting Alistair be in command.

It was obvious which ship was for them. It sat in the middle of the bay, directly above a launch hole. The two side doors were open, and when Alistair stepped in, he saw the earpiece.

He snapped it into place as he sat in the pilot's chair.

Nero took his spot next to Alistair. "Let us hope you fly this better than the last ship."

"This is why they pay me the big bucks, Nero. I use my brain. AI, can you hear me?"

"Affirmative."

"Can you fly this thing if I tell you where I want you to land it?" Alistair asked.

"Affirmative. I have extensive training on all ships aboard the dreadnought."

Alistair looked at Nero and winked. "Okay, I want you to get us to the coordinates I'm typing in now." His hands rapidly hit the screens in front of him, putting in the target as the compound. Once he got there, he'd figure out the rest.

"Location confirmed. Are we ready for launch?" the AI asked.

"Affirmative."

There was a brief pause before the AI came back. "I believe you were trying to make a joke at my expense. I will not dignify it with a response."

Alistair smiled. *I think I'm gonna like this one.*

The launch hole opened beneath them, and the ship went through two chambers until it reached an air-sealed one.

It turned vertically so Alistair was staring at the deck. Another circular hole opened in front of him, and just before the engines fired, Alistair said, "Don't hold anything back. Full speed."

"Affirmative."

Faitrin hadn't said everything she wanted to when she'd spoken to Thoreaux in the war room. She'd said what needed to be said for the room, but not for Thoreaux. Now, as the first man was just about in range of her lasers, she knew she needed to.

It was a stupid decision; she knew that as well, but she also knew she might not get another chance. Prometheus was a god among men, but even gods failed.

If he failed, they all failed.

Her eyes were grayed over; she was harmonized with her ship.

Jeeves, she said with her mind, *connect me to Thoreaux.*

Connected, madam.

Faitrin spoke quickly. She was going to miss the shot she should have taken, but she had to get this out.

These past four or five months with you have been the scariest and best of my life. I love you, and I want you to know that. We're going to make it out of this, but if for some reason, I don't, know that I will love you until the end of time. Until all the stars explode and the universe's expansion stops, I'll love you, Thoreaux. If there's something after this life, with the gods, I'll love you there too. Thank you for everything you've given me.

Jeeves cut the transmission.

She told the AI one last thing. *Don't let any transmissions from him come to me until I give permission.*

Yes, madam.

She needed complete focus because a metric ton of murderous creatures had just entered her airspace.

Eyes gray, hands still, she opened fire with her mind. The first man-filled capsule exploded as the lasers hit it, and her corvette peeled to the right. There was no shortage of targets. The real concern was making sure *she* didn't get smacked by one of those falling pricks.

It had been some time since she'd piloted like this, and she'd forgotten how much she missed dogfights. Her brain had been modified in a way that allowed her to simultaneously steer, adjust speed and trajectory, and aim. The better the pilot, the better they could do all those things at the same time.

Faitrin was a damn good pilot.

She cut the corvette left as a capsule nearly impaled it. She adjusted the lasers with a thought, aiming them to the right of her ship.

A second later, the capsule was in flames.

Weaving around the capsules, she slowly adjusted her altitude, still firing the lasers. In the distance, she could see other pilots doing the same.

Jeeves spoke through their harmony. *We are down one corvette. Their fighter pilots have breached the capital. You can expect incoming fire from all directions.*

Noted, she responded as she fired at a cluster of falling capsules. Four more enemies burned alive. Without speaking, she told Jeeves she wanted to broadcast to the entire fleet—if this small a group could be called that. *We're down* one. *Make sure the next one that goes isn't you. If possible, remain close to the ground-to-air defense system. I'll take care of the perimeter.*

The transmission ended, and Faitrin hit the throttle hard. She watched as her team pulled in.

She was going to circle the city and force the invaders to the center.

If they could get them all in a single, large cluster, it'd be a lot easier to annihilate them.

It didn't matter who you were.

Being launched into space, then breaching a planet's atmosphere—all within the confines of a human-sized pill—brought issues.

Even for a queen.

Cristin vomited into the capsule as the force of her speed rocked her body. The vomit disrupted her vision as it smeared across her helmet's faceplate. She couldn't wipe it off since she couldn't move while the capsule was in motion.

What she *could* see made her happy.

The sky was full of falling soldiers. The red streaks they left in the air looked like victory parade ribbons.

She saw black corvettes soaring through the sky, their lasers raining on buildings and humans alike.

The fall was fast, though it felt excruciatingly long.

Finally, the capsule sensed the ground and began using the thrusters aligned along its body to adjust speed.

It touched down, laying longways so Cristin's face was

looking at the sky. The transparent door opened, and the Ice Queen grabbed the edges and pulled herself out. She ripped her helmet off her head and tossed it on the ground.

She fell to her knees and vomited once more, mostly spit and stomach acid. This wasn't her first time in a capsule launch, but godsdamn, did she hate it.

Cristin was efficient at changing from the capsule suit to her armor. One could fall in a personal payload delivery ship without needing a special suit. Not so in a capsule.

She wasn't sure what she'd seen back on the dreadnought. She wasn't even sure what happened. The man was more than human, and Cristin had never experienced anything like it.

He'd had the advantage up there, and Cristin was not so prideful that she couldn't redirect the battle. He'd missed his opportunity, and *she* now had the advantage.

Before putting on her helmet, she placed the comm chip in her ear.

"Simo, are you here or still up there?"

"What in the actual fuck just happened?" the man fired back.

"It doesn't matter now. It's over. The war's begun, and that's all any of us need to focus on. Now, are you here, or are you still up there?"

"Gods damn you, Cristin. Galer and I are both down here. He's to the north, and I got fucked up and ended up south. Neither of us knew if some kind of virus had infected your systems. Still don't. If I die out here, I promise my son will come for you."

The Ice Queen hardly heard his threats. They both

needed to be here. Regardless of their weaknesses, the men were powerful warriors when they wanted to be.

"Listen to me carefully," she said as she pulled her weapon from its holster. "The man who took this planet is not human. I don't know what he is or how he does what he does. If you see him, do not engage unless you can overwhelm or surprise him. If you *don't* listen to me, you'll die. Tell Galer the same."

A brief pause, then, "What are you saying?"

"If you get to the battle, I imagine you'll see firsthand. I left him up in the dreadnought, but there's no way he stayed up there. He'll be here with us shortly if he isn't already. I can't explain it because I don't understand it, but you'll see. Just remember, don't engage him one-on-one." She paused, one other important thing coming to mind. "If he dies, this thing is over."

"Fine, I'll tell Galer. Where are you?"

The Ice Queen flicked her wrist up. "Location." The watch shot up a holographic view of the city and her spot in it.

"I'm east of the capitol." She looked into the sky and saw a corvette above her and about a kilometer away. It appeared to be circling the city. "I think what they're trying to do, Simo, is force us into the middle. If I were him, that's where I'd go. He may need armor, and his generals will be there strategizing. Meet in the center."

"It'll make us sitting relpins."

"How many men will you lose to win this planet, Simo?"

Another pause. "A lot."

"Me too. We have to overwhelm him. If he's there and

his forces are in an outside circle, he'll be in the middle of us with little help. We'll lose many, but we'll have a chance to overwhelm him. We beat him, we win a planet."

"Okay. I hope you're right. I'll tell Galer the same. See you soon, ice bitch."

The connection ended.

Cristin looked at her watch. "Congregation of forces."

Another hologram of the city, this time red dots both flying and on the ground filled it. The forces had mostly landed north and west due to where their ships had stopped. The plan had been to surround the city, but this would work too.

It gave the Ice Queen almost a straight shot to the capitol building.

She reached down and engaged her shoes, then took a stride to make sure the anti-gravity tech hadn't been damaged and bounded ten meters forward.

The Ice Queen started her march.

Caesar heard Servia's voice in his comm. Five weird dead creatures lay at his feet. The battle had moved away from him, so he had a moment to listen. His eyes narrowed as he peered at the strange creatures fighting his brothers.

"Strategy has shifted. All troops need to understand this. The enemy is congregated north and west right now, but they're disorganized. Whatever Prometheus did up there messed up what we thought their original plans were. Air support is going to push as hard as it can to get them in the middle. *Let them do their job.* All ground support's job is to form a perimeter and assist in that movement. Kill as many as you can, but don't get trapped inside. I'm moving our heavy artillery to assist with the perimeter. Once there, we'll cut down as many as possible."

There was no mention of Prometheus' location. Perhaps she didn't know. Caesar reached up and switched his comm channel to the warriors in his purview. He spoke in the gigantes' guttural language, explaining the plan.

The lines where the buildings stood were about a half-kilometer away. He'd been stupid to come out this far, but he'd simply started marching until he found people to kill. The buildings would give the gigantes the ability to maneuver without fighting.

Caesar was a warrior, not a strategist. He understood that. He also knew Servia would be nearly defenseless in that building. The AllMother too.

Plans had changed, so his would too. She needed help, and that was where he was going. The rest could hold the perimeter.

The gigante, holding two sabers, started his march back from where he'd come from. If Servia died, he would too, but she wouldn't die alone.

Caesar formed a thought in his native tongue but translated it as he went forward.

Prometheus, if you're out there, we need you.

Thoreaux couldn't hear Servia since he was currently in a losing match against some kind of Sasquatch.

The white-furred creature grabbed him by his armored neck and tossed him.

Thoreaux was wearing Fire Starter armor from the Terram, but even so, he was overwhelmed.

He rose in a high arc and came back down five meters from the Sasquatch. It had a human head and hair, but everything else was animal. Thoreaux took a knee, not thinking about what had just come over his comm. If he didn't get out of this situation, he was dead

The animal didn't seem to have any weapons. Maybe they'd been lost in the frantic war, but it handled itself just fine without them.

Thoreaux's MechPulse was ten meters in the opposite direction. He had a beam in a holster, but he hadn't drawn it.

The animal was looking at him as if deciding something. The human eyes showed no fear, only cunning and a need to kill.

Thoreaux's speed would never be up to Pro's, but he was still fast. He drew the weapon and fired with both hands gripping the weapon, standing and moving closer as he did.

If Thoreaux was fast, the creature was blazing. It launched left, and the first shot hit its ribs. It landed on its left leg, then launched right and forward.

Thoreaux tracked it with his beam, firing the entire time but unable to keep up.

The space between them was shortening fast, then he'd be in its grip again.

He hit the trigger three more times, then the animal was on top of him. It forced Thoreaux onto his back, breaking his grip on the beam and sending it skittering across the pavement. They were in the middle of an intersection, four buildings at the corners. The sounds of explosions and glass breaking were everywhere. Smoke rose from buildings and streets alike.

The creature's hands had dagger-like claws, and it started ripping at the armor, trying to find a weakness in the technology. Thoreaux was scrambling with his hands, trying to beat back the animal, but the thing was just too fast.

It grabbed his helmet with one hand, then started bashing it against the pavement. The first blow put stars in Thoreaux's eyes as the asphalt beneath him broke. The second put black clouds around the edges of his sight.

The creature was gone. Thoreaux lay on the street, blinking inside his helmet. He didn't understand anything and was just trying to keep from blacking out.

An armored hand was suddenly in front of him.

"Broth, I wonder if Faitrin will kiss me when I bring back your scalp still attached to your head?"

A second hand came down, and Thoreaux was lifted to his feet.

Relm stood in front of him, also wearing a Fire Starter. He snapped his fingers in front of Thoreaux's face a few times. "You tracking?"

Thoreaux looked to his left. The animal was at the edge of the intersection, his head a mixture of bone and plasma.

"Broth, you tracking?"

"Gods, what are those things?" Thoreaux said, unable to look away from the dead animal.

"I don't know, but I need you functional." Relm lightly

slapped Thoreaux's helmet, jerking his attention back. "You tracking?"

"Tracking."

"Good." Relm turned and looked at the capitol building in the center. "New plan. We need to decide if we want to follow it. Servia says to fall back and form a perimeter, forcing those things and any people inside it. Air support and the whole nine."

Thoreaux was starting to understand words again as his vision cleared. He followed Relm's look at the capitol.

"She's in there alone," Relm continued. "So is the AllMother. We disobey orders, we're going to weaken the perimeter. We don't, those things will eat them both alive."

Thoreaux had almost caught up.

Relm still wasn't looking at him but gazing into the distance as if the answer could be found in the glass windows of the skyscraper. "I vote we go back. Either way, I think we're fucked, but if I'm going to die, I'd rather do it with people I know. Going out like you almost did doesn't look too appealing."

Thoreaux took a deep breath, shaking off what had just happened and replacing it with rage. "Did you relay those orders to the gigantes?"

Glass broke and fell from a building behind them. Relm swirled with his MechPulse raised toward the sound. He held the position for a second, then brought the weapon down. "Come on."

The two trotted down the street toward the building on their right. "Yeah. It's been relayed. That's why the streets are emptying. We're retreating to the perimeter."

"Servia's about to sacrifice herself to try to salvage this," Thoreaux said. "I'm not letting her do it."

"Yeah, to hell with that. They'll write songs about her bravery when it's over, and that just can't happen. We'll never live it down."

Thoreaux looked at Relm. "Are you ever serious?"

Relm shook his head. "Nah. Stress kills. Let's go."

The two started their march to save those they loved.

CHAPTER SEVENTEEN

Alistair was regretting having told the AI to get them there fast. The AI was more advanced than he'd thought, and he had almost vomited at its maneuvers.

Nero had vomited, then yelled in his guttural language.

Alistair didn't ask for a translation.

The ship touched down on the top of the capitol building. During the flight, Alistair had done his best to understand the layout of the battle. He wasn't sure about what he'd seen, but there appeared to be movement toward a perimeter. He had no idea and didn't have time to consider it.

"We have arrived," the AI said through the comm.

"Can you stick with me for a little longer?" Alistair asked.

"Affirmative."

The door to the ship opened and Obs hopped out, obviously glad to be clear of it.

Nero went to the right and Alistair to the left. Alistair

jogged to the other side. "I need armor, and I need to talk to Thoreaux. Did your dream show this?"

Nero looked at the vomit all over his armor. "It didn't show that." He looked up. "I know only two things more from the dream. Servia is in command, and this is where you were supposed to end up."

Alistair could tell something was wrong with the giant. Time was short, but he hadn't seen the touched gigante look like this before. "What's going on? And don't be coy; there isn't time for it."

The giant tilted his head toward the sky. "I wasn't here in the dream. I never made it down. I died up there."

"Ha!" Alistair shouted and slapped Nero on the shoulder. "Wind and fate and all that shit, we still decide how it ends up. Let's go."

The two rushed to the stairs and went down two levels to the war room.

Servia was alone in it, and she turned around as they entered.

Obs bounded to her and grabbed her hand lightly with his jaws. Dried blood fell off his maw in flecks as he pulled away.

She saw Alistair, and tears filled her eyes. "*Ave*, you son of a bitch."

Alistair gave her a giant hug. "*Ave*, Servia." He pushed her back and let his arms drop. "Jeeves, can you get my armor up here? Anyone still in the building to do it?"

"It was summoned the moment you entered the building, sir. It's approximately two minutes away. As an aside, I must request you never ask me to copilot with you again."

"Everybody's got jokes," Alistair said. He looked at

Servia. "Give me the rundown."

She unloaded as quickly as she could, and his mind latched onto it all at once. He also understood what she'd been doing to herself. "Just going to die up here, you and the old woman?"

"It's our best chance. Or was. What do we do?"

A short, stout young man pushed a cart into the room. The armor lay across it.

Alistair walked over and the young man turned to leave, but Alistair put a hand on his shoulder to stop him. "Jeeves, how many people are in the building?"

"Twenty. The one in here is the only one I would recommend to assist."

Alistair looked at the young man. "What's your name?"

"Brillin, sir."

"You from Pluto? You were there when it burned? An original Subversive?" The last word came out mocking what he'd used to call those he now commanded.

"Yes, sir."

"You know who I am?"

"*Ave*, Prometheus," Brillin whispered.

Alistair looked at Servia. "Let's get him some armor and a MechPulse. He's strong enough to wield it."

Jeeves spoke. "Sir, some of our soldiers are refusing orders."

Alistair's eyes narrowed. "What are they doing?"

"Entering," Jeeves said.

Alistair turned toward the sound of footsteps in the doorway, having no clue what was happening.

"You bastards," Servia cursed. "You heard my orders!"

Alistair was staring at his brothers. Thoreaux was in the

middle, Relm to his left, and Caesar on the right.

Relm was smiling. "Well, isn't this a reunion? Who spiked the punch?"

Servia was across the room in a flash and slapped Thoreaux's face hard. His cheek flushed red around a white outline of her hand. "You were given an *order*. Form the perimeter. Now it's weaker."

Tears flooded her eyes again.

The armor on Thoreaux's hand retracted into the wrist. He reached up and lightly touched her face. "You and I have been together since adulthood. The perimeter will be fine, and if it's not, you're not dying alone."

The tears fell from her eyes and she leaned forward, hugging the armored warrior. She held on for a few seconds before pulling back and moving next to Alistair.

The former Titan touched the armor next to him. He was quiet for a second, and when he spoke, he didn't look up. "The plan remains. The perimeter will cut them down from the outside."

He looked up.

"We are the center. We will hold. No one is dying, alone or together."

He looked at their faces and realized something else: they were each other's great wind, carrying each other when things grew too heavy to bear. "We will *hold*. Five of us and this new man will hold the center. It isn't a coincidence that we're all here now. Everything worked together to bring us here, and on the AllMother's soul, we are going to *hold*. Everything that comes will break against this center. Do you all understand that?"

Silent and solemn nods were the response.

"Jeeves, show me the battlefield."

A giant hologram filled the table in the center of the room. Green dots formed a ragged quarter-circle around the north and west portions. Red dots were intertwined with the green, but for the most part, the red was being pushed toward the capitol building in the center.

Alistair studied the map for a moment. "Any idea how long until they reach us?"

"At current rates of battle and movement of the perimeter in, I'd put it at ten minutes."

The plan formed in Alistair's head. "Servia, you're in command. Keep us updated on movement patterns and where the attacks are coming from. Thoreaux, Nero, Obs, you're with me. Caesar, Relm, Brillin, you're Team Two. We don't leave the building. We are the rock they break against as the perimeter tightens. Everyone understand?"

"Got it, broth," Relm said for everyone.

Alistair knew he couldn't revert to his usual tactic of running headfirst into this. There were too many red dots in that hologram. His attributes wouldn't save them. He knew what was important.

"There's one woman who matters. She's this flock's true shepherd, the creator of those beasts outside. We kill her, we break their back. You'll know her when you see her since her body looks like she should be nowhere near a war zone and her spirit says she was birthed in one. Trust me, you'll know what I mean. When you see her, that's who you kill."

Alistair's mind was processing things at a rapid pace. He grabbed his armor and started putting it on as he spoke, his hands moving like a skilled surgeon's.

"Caesar, your team takes the lower half of the building. We take the upper half. These people have the technology to attack from both parts, and that's how we're going to split it up."

He closed everything but his right wrist and hand.

Jeeves spoke. "Five minutes until contact, sir."

Alistair knelt and the others followed, even Brillin understanding that something important was about to happen.

Relm pulled a blade from his belt and handed it to the newcomer. "Pro doesn't fuck around, kid, and you're about to see it up close. Do as he does, say what he says, and when the time comes, draw your blood."

Brillin took the knife carefully.

Alistair was looking at none of them. He stared at the floor. When he closed his eyes for one second, Luna's face passed through his mind.

This isn't the end, he thought, *because I haven't seen you again. It doesn't end until that happens, my love.*

"I do not kill for glory. I do not kill for malice. I kill because it is right. Because if I do not kill, those who seek to harm me and those I love will do so."

For Alistair, there was no one else in the room. He was alone. As he brought the blade to his arm, he relinquished control, and Prometheus came forward.

He sliced a circular line around his arm. The blood ran down his forearm and dripped on the floor.

"I do not fear the enemy. I do not fear death. I only fear living without protecting those I love. I only fear cowardice and hiding from my duty. As this blood flows, so will I. I bleed now so that I will not later. I bleed now so that those who sow harm against me know that blood does not frighten me. I bleed now because it is this blood that will conquer anyone in my path. See it and fear. See it and die."

The blade hit the floor, and Prometheus put his right hand on his dripping left arm. Wiping blood from the wound, he spread it under each eye.

I'm coming, Luna. Hold on for me. It won't be long.

Pro looked at faces smeared with blood.

They spoke as one. "*Ave*, Prometheus."

The Ice Queen stood a hundred meters from the capitol building. She saw her warriors and others fighting, though there weren't many. They were mainly circling the other side, but they would flood this way soon.

The other two warlords were approaching her. Fat Galer looked like a wrecking ball in his armor. Simo's black armor made him look like Death.

"You fucked this all up, Cristin," Simo said as he reached her.

"You know how many years it's been since I fought?" Galer asked, though he sounded happy to be in battle again.

The three looked at the towering building.

"How do you want to do it, Cristin? You got us down here, so I hope you have a plan."

She'd thought about it during the march, and she did have a strategy. It might get the other two warlords killed, but it was likely to ensure that *her* family grew stronger.

These two could not understand what they would face without seeing him in action. Even now, she imagined these men thought themselves stronger than everyone else down here. They were fools, and if they died, it would be their fault.

Her family was what mattered, and Cristin would never forget that.

"Did you see the ship land on top of the building?"

"Yeah. Looked like one of yours," Galer answered.

"It was, and Kane made perhaps the dumbest decision he's ever made. He kept my AI attached to him. I know their entire plan, and it revolves around that building. His core team is in there, and they plan on breaking us by not giving up that tower while their soldiers continue to push us against it."

Simo looked at her with wide eyes. "You're serious?"

Cristin nodded without taking her eyes off the building. "The entire group just did some ritual."

Listening to that man say those words was the first time she'd ever had a chill of fear roll down her spine. That was something she would never speak of. Powerful he might be, but he'd already given her the victory and didn't even know it.

"Us three are going into that tower, and we're going to do it quietly. There's only a handful of them in there, and they can't cover the entire area. It's impossible. I'm going to know where they're all the time, as long as he keeps my AI in his ear. We'll go to where they're not, then we'll get our men inside. Once he dies, the rest will break."

"In all my life," Galer said with wonder, "I've never

heard of such an idiotic move. He's already dead, just doesn't know it yet."

Even Simo had nothing smart to say.

The Ice Queen smiled. "Simo, your men are lower third. Galer, you're middle. I'm taking the top. We'll end this in thirty minutes."

Caesar and Relm made the decision that they wouldn't split up. The newcomer hadn't shied away from cutting his arm, but that didn't mean he was prepared for what was to come.

They would be a boulder that rolled through the lower half of the building, crushing everything in its path.

They started in the lobby. The glass surrounding it was reinforced, and though they knew it would break, the enemy would be forced through the entry doors in the beginning.

The gigante and the two men were spread at even ten meters across the lobby. Relm held his MechPulse in front of him. Brillin did the same, looking uncomfortable with the weapon.

A ring of humans and those strange hybrids was moving closer to the building. The battle was about forty meters out from it, but the perimeter was continuing to tighten. Servia had updated them that out of the ten corvettes they'd started with, only five remained. She'd told them Faitrin was the Prometheus of the sky, however. For every corvette the enemy had taken out, they'd taken ten of theirs.

Caesar was silent as he stood in his black armor. He stared out the windows, watching the battle move closer.

A corvette swooped low and blasted a row of hybrids. Huge chunks of rock and earth exploded into the air, and the ship swirled away. That was Faitrin, doing her best to hold the center.

Relm stood in the middle of the three and looked in Brillin's direction. "How old are ya, kid?"

Sweat was dripping from the young man's face, smearing the blood in long streaks down his cheeks. "Seventeen," he replied without looking over.

"Hey, not bad, not bad. First time I picked up my Mech-Pulse and went to battle, I was sixteen." He tapped the weapon in front of him like it was a beloved pet. "How much time you got with that thing? Had any practice?"

"I was training back on Pluto," Brillin said, trying to make his voice loud enough to cover the distance. Caesar heard the shaking in it. "There wasn't any training with the Terram."

"That's more than I had," Relm said. Caesar understood what he was doing and was glad about it. The gigante couldn't connect on a friendly level; his life hadn't allowed him to develop that skill. Relm had it in spades. "Kid, I'm gonna be honest with you. I'm a fucking surgeon with this thing. You put me in a pulse battle with just about anyone, including that god-like bastard Prometheus, and I got at least a fifty-fifty shot of coming out alive."

Sweat dripped from Brillin's face to the floor.

"Hey, kid, look at me."

Brillin turned his head to the right.

"You're about to see the GOAT of MechPulses go into

battle. You know what the GOAT is?"

He shook his head.

"'Greatest of all time.' You look like you don't realize the front row seat you're getting today. People would pay a lot of credits to watch what I'm about to do. Not to mention, this big bumbling monster to my right is going to put on a killing clinic."

Relm had forced a smile out of the young man.

"Now, all bullshit aside, we got two to three minutes before those fucks outside decide hiding in here is better than being blasted by corvettes, so listen and listen well. The reason I'm so good is this? The MechPulse is not my weapon, it's an extension of me. It's the same as my arm or hand, and I use it as I would them. It does what *I* want, not the other way around. Say it with me, okay?"

Brillin nodded.

"My weapon is my arm."

Sounding stronger, Brillin repeated it. "My weapon is my arm."

"Good. Another piece of advice. The big bastard on my right is about thirty seconds away from pulling out his sabers and cutting down anything that comes in here. Do not hit him with your godsdamn arm. Or me, for that matter."

Relm closed his faceplate and turned forward.

The enemy was looking at the glass. Fire roared in the streets. Shattered glass and rocks lay everywhere.

Caesar grabbed the two hilts on either side of his belt and stepped forward. He didn't look over as he spoke. His voice boomed across the lobby. "Kill them all. Every fucking one."

Five hybrids rushed the door, the only piece of glass not reinforced.

They crashed through as if it were paper.

Caesar's right foot stretched out, then he was running. He'd heard of these creatures out in the galaxy. He'd had masters scream at him that those things were better killers and he could get twice as many for half the price.

His footfalls sounded like rocks falling from the heavens as he rushed forward. The words of those masters rang through his mind with each falling stone.

They're better.

You're nothing.

A waste of money.

They don't even need weapons to do what you do.

The hybrids leaped as one.

Caesar's sabers fell from the hilts, green lasers searing the air they cut through. He extended both arms as the first two hybrids reached him.

The lasers went through their chests, but he didn't stop there. Caesar kept rushing to the door, then thrust the dying hybrids off his sabers and back into the street.

The remaining three had missed their jumps and were turning to him since he was the immediate threat.

Caesar faced them, seeing Relm cross the lobby to put more space between him and Brillin.

He spun the sabers in his hands.

Relm's pulse fired twice and the plasma wracked the hybrid's bodies, burning through fur and flesh. Brillin fired his and missed the first time, wide right.

The hybrid turned as it realized the threat behind it.

"*AGAIN!*" Relm shouted, his voice as ruthless as Caesar had ever heard it.

The kid fired again, and plasma coated the front of the hybrid.

Caesar crossed the distance between him and the enemy in two huge steps, then raked his sabers across the burning creatures rolling on the ground.

"Five down," Relm called from the back of the lobby. "A few thousand more to go. It ain't nothing to a gangster, kid."

Caesar turned, sabers pointed toward the floor. The dead lay at his feet; it was the greatest monument he could build to honor his leader.

On this day, Caesar planned to build a big monument.

———

The AllMother emerged from her room and went to the war room. She was stretching herself to the limit, and she knew it. She could feel Prometheus again, though he was in the building.

She had to help.

The cost didn't matter.

Servia stood in front of the table, her hands moving holovids around while she barked questions at Jeeves and orders at soldiers.

The AllMother said nothing, only walked up and stood next to her at the table.

"What are you doing here, Mother?" Servia snapped.

The AllMother studied the maps while her ancient mind raced through the building, coming to an understanding of where it was being attacked, where they were strongest, and where they were weakest.

"I can't look after you and focus. You've gotta go back and lay down."

The AllMother didn't take her eyes off the maps or lose her focus. "Girl, I've laid more men and women under the ground than everyone here combined. You let me worry about me. You worry about making sure my children know how to win."

The AllMother's mind was giving her what she wanted, call it overdrive, an extra gear, or willpower; it didn't matter. She didn't feel as she had at twenty-five, but gods, it was close.

And that?

That felt good.

She didn't need to see Servia smile at her snap. She felt it.

The AllMother had built her legacy out of necessity so people would follow her insane quest. She'd never cared about fame. That hadn't been the driving force, not for a single day. Now, though, standing next to one of her daughters, she realized this might be the last time she ever did this.

If that was the case, anyone who survived would remember her.

Perhaps a little fame wasn't too bad.

She smiled, and her mind reached out to her protégé.

Prometheus, you about gave me whiplash when you sent that message. Let's see if I can do the same to you.

Prometheus suddenly stopped walking.

Obs skidded across the floor as he halted, sensing something had changed. Thoreaux stopped a meter behind, and Nero went a bit farther before realizing everyone else had frozen.

"Damn," Pro whispered.

He didn't know how much force the old woman had thrown that with, but it'd buckled his knees. He couldn't imagine the power she must've possessed as a young woman.

Pro looked at Obs. "I'm fine. The old woman just entered the battlefield, and I think she means to be a factor."

Heard loud and clear, Mother.

He realized that was the first time he'd ever called her that.

Let's not do that next time because you might get me killed, he told her.

I trust you, she said, *but I'm probably the only one in here who knows what's in your ear. Please tell me you know what's in your ear and that there's a reason for it.*

The other three were staring at him. They couldn't see through his faceplate, but he was smiling.

Trust me like I do you, he responded.

Done. What do you need from me? I don't have long, I know that, but the time I do have is going to be impactful.

I've got my part covered, he said. *Do everything you can to keep the rest of the council alive. I'll keep myself alive.*

Ave, Prometheus, the old woman told him before ending their connection.

Obs trotted over to sit in front of his master. He looked

up with worry in his eyes.

Pro retracted the faceplate to show his smile. "I'm good, ya worryin' fool. I don't know how she's doing it, but the AllMother is helping." He looked at Nero. "Can you feel her?"

The giant considered the question, then said, "Something is different."

"It's her."

Servia came over the comm inside his helmet. "Pro, something's changing outside. The battle against the perimeter is slacking, and we've got transport vehicles coming to the roof."

"How's the perimeter handling the fight?"

"We're down four artillery, have two left. Best-case scenario, we've lost thirty percent of our soldiers. They might be down ten percent. We're down two more corvettes."

"Faitrin?" he asked.

"Goddess of the skies. Still killing."

He had one more question. "What's Jeeves' estimate of the number coming to the roof?"

There was a pause on the comm. "It's bad. You've got one hundred landing now. We think another transport is bringing another hundred."

"We're on it. Out."

"Pro!" she shouted. "That's too many even for you."

"Know anyone you'd rather get up there? We can give them a call."

"No one in this universe or any others." Another pause, and when she spoke, she projected the confidence of a general. "Good luck, and stay alive."

"Keep the perimeter's deaths as low as you can, Serv. This is going to be over soon. Out."

The connection ended. Prometheus squatted next to Obs and put his armored arm gently around the drathe. He knew the animal's ribs were broken from when he'd found the Whip. Obs hadn't whined or shown any signs of pain. The animal was a warrior. Alistair looked up at Nero. "We're going to the roof. All I need is for you three to stay alive. We've got Nero's nanotech to help with wounds, and Obs, I know you're hurt. Don't overextend yourself up there. Thoreaux, try to keep control of yourself. We've got up to two hundred enemies landing on the roof. We're going to get that number to a manageable prospect, but please trust me. All of you. No matter what, stay alive."

He knew they didn't understand why he was saying these things. All he could do was hope they listened to that one directive.

Prometheus stood, and his faceplate locked into place.

He stepped past them.

One thought went through his mind.

The center will hold.

The Ice Queen had separated from the other warlords. Her watch had shown her the building's blueprints. Multiple staircases went from basement to roof, as well as an elevator. Cristin understood that meeting Kane alone in any staircase would be the end of her, and consequently, her family.

The AI had been able to tell her where he was the entire time, though.

Talking into her comm, she asked, "Does he know you're still there? Does he have any idea you're listening?"

"This answer cannot be a short one. Do you want to hear it?"

The AI had learned early that Cristin expected to-the-point answers without a lot of filler. If the answer was long, it was because it had to be.

"Go," she commanded.

"I cannot say with one hundred percent positivity. I believe he was impressed by my abilities, and based on personality analysis, there was a high probability he thought he could communicate with you through me, which is possible, as you know. I'm able to measure his heart rate and blood pressure through the comm, both of which are remarkably low and have been the entire time. If they were higher, I'd say his physical and mental state had led him to forget. A small percentage of humans have a natural inclination to their central nervous system not reacting in large swings. If that is the case, then based on human psychology in wartime, I'd put it at a seventy-five-percent chance that he's forgotten. If he isn't worried or stressed, there's a ninety-five-percent chance he's a psychopath and a twenty-percent chance he's forgotten."

Cristin's nails dug into her palm. Twenty to a seventy-five percent chance that he'd forgotten, or an eighty to twenty-five percent chance that this was some kind of strategy.

Psychopath or a natural inclination?

She had to make a choice and quickly. The troops were landing.

Standing in the empty stairwell, she shook her head. He wasn't a psychopath. The man cared too much about his family and people who were not his family to be a psychopath. His body simply didn't freak out, which most likely meant he'd forgotten.

The image of his barely controlled corvette in that dogfight filled her mind. He didn't plan. He acted. That was what he was doing now.

Two hundred soldiers and she was one of them.

This was the ambush she needed.

Cristin rarely questioned her decisions after she made them, but she understood this man was *different.*

"Let me know any updates immediately. I'm going to the roof."

The AI said nothing in acknowledgment, just as Cristin wanted it.

She took the stairs slowly. She doubted if her soldiers could kill the man, but tire him? Weaken him?

Certainly.

Nanotech swarmed through the air, tiny bug-like creatures looking for allies' injuries.

Nero had damn near emptied himself of them the moment he'd stepped onto the roof. Prometheus understood the physical toll that took on the gigante. He also knew Nero had done it because he understood the most important directive.

Stay alive.

It wasn't the nanotech Prometheus saw now, but the multitude of black-armored humans and fur-covered hybrids trying to kill him.

His mind blanketed the roof while his body moved across it as if he had no physical form.

He could have been a mage of old, his Whip the wand that performed his magic. His amplified strength had reached unknown levels with the Fire Starter. The hybrids came for him, most not holding weapons, some having sabers.

It didn't matter.

He cut them down like blades of grass.

His mind was where the battle truly was. He needed to know two things: Obs, Nero, and Thoreaux were alive, and when that bitch was coming up here. Mentally, he could toss a lot of the enemy over the edge, but he needed their cover to ensure the shepherd arrived.

Nero was five meters from him and was constantly under threat of being overwhelmed. His rage from earlier was back; the giant seemed to be angry that he *hadn't* died and was taking that massive disappointment out on anyone in front of him.

Still, there were too many. The nanotech was covering him to heal deep gashes and penetrations. Pro constantly had to cut his way to the giant and stand back to back with him until the number dwindled.

Obs was racing around the perimeter like a sheepdog from Earth. He was careful with his attacks, moving in when he saw an opening and darting back out just as quickly. Thoreaux was taking a similar approach, and

Prometheus couldn't have been prouder of his second. He was holding onto his rage and picking them off from the outside. He'd left Pro and Nero to be the tanks in the middle, but Pro couldn't have saved Nero *and* Thoreaux.

Another transport was coming with another hundred soldiers in it. The bitch was trying to drown them.

The giant was weakening, his pure rage unable to keep up with the damage his body was taking.

Pro started toward him again. He might not survive another separation.

A human soldier leveled a rifle at Pro. His Whip slashed the man's right leg off, and he fell to the knee of his left while screaming. Pro jumped and used the dying man's shoulder to launch into the air.

He came down behind a hybrid that had his claws deep in Nero's shoulders.

The creature came apart, his lower body falling to the roof.

Nero shoved the upper half off him.

The giant turned, knowing what to do.

The transport flew above them. It wasn't going to land this time, so the soldiers dropped from the air. Small parachutes were attached to their shoulders and arms. When they spread their arms wide, the wind lowered them safely. Ten dropped at a time.

Prometheus decided to try something, his reckless side unable to be kept at bay.

He tossed the Whip into the air with as much force as he could. The lasers started to retract since his touch was gone, but not before they impaled one of the falling soldiers.

Prometheus ducked a hybrid's clawed swipe and mentally rushed the Whip back to his hand.

It came to life, and the hybrid fell.

He heard Nero yell from behind him and turned. The giant was on one knee, a human's saber having sliced halfway through his right leg. The nanotech swarmed, but Pro knew time was running out.

His Whip lashed out and took off the human's head.

That was when he felt it—the stairwell door opening at the far corner of the building.

The Ice Queen had arrived.

Pro stepped in front of the fallen gigante. The AI would be able to tell Pro was speaking to it. He'd studied the thing for this very reason. "AI, connect with your queen."

He heard the click, then said one word.

"Welcome."

He was facing her direction. Obs and Thoreaux were out of the way, Nero behind him. He lunged forward, and his mind rushed toward her.

People and hybrids fell out of the way as if a wave of fire were ripping through the air. Those near the edge fell, and those flying above were blitzed upward, their tiny parachutes helpless to save them on their next fall. The transport's engines couldn't combat the force, and it too was thrust away from the building before beginning a fatal fall.

A tunnel formed between him and her.

The fighting ceased. All stared at their queen and her challenger.

Still connected through the comm, Prometheus said, "Let's see who can save their family."

CHAPTER EIGHTEEN

The AllMother's mind was everywhere in the building but the roof. She'd tried to go up there too, ignoring Pro's orders, but his power had covered it, and she found it too tiring to push through.

The battle on the other floors was more than enough.

The enemy's numbers were staggering, and she knew their warlords were all in the building. They were calling all their troops now, sensing the end was near. The perimeter was falling, the corvettes unable to help because of lack of numbers.

They knew her shepherd was inside now, and they were coming to kill him.

Caesar's group had had to retreat. They were still alive, although the AllMother sensed the giant's fatigue. His nanotech was healing him, although he was mostly just exhausted from being the brute force. The young man had taken a shoulder hit.

Relm was the only one not hurt, but the AllMother knew he was tired.

She wasn't what she once was, but the old woman was doing what she could.

As they retreated deeper into the building, the enemies now too many to fight head-on, she opened doors and then held them shut as long as possible. The nanotech did its work, and it gave them time for a few breaths.

Eventually, though, the hordes broke through.

The AllMother used everything in her arsenal to assist. Lighting fixtures fell from ceilings, killing or paralyzing those beneath. Chairs and desks flew at high speeds and pulverized bone when they made contact.

Servia worked next to her. Jeeves' voice constantly gave them new information.

"Perimeter down to forty percent. Estimated time before collapse ten minutes."

Servia leaned forward on the table. "There's too many."

The AllMother wanted to weep from exhaustion. She looked at her daughter and placed a hand on her shoulder. "He's going to deliver us. Keep going."

Servia gazed at her with desperation on her face.

The AllMother staggered away from the table, her hand falling from Servia's shoulder.

Servia whipped around to grab the woman, but it was too late. The AllMother hit the floor. Servia was over her in a second, but the AllMother's face made her stop.

It was Prometheus' mind.

He'd found the shepherd.

He would deliver them, or they would die right here, right now. Nothing else mattered.

With the last of her strength, she sent a message to the other three warriors.

To the roof. All of you.

Only Caesar's strength kept him on his feet.

The two humans first stumbled and then fell to the floor. Relm was on his ass, Brillin on all fours.

Caesar's monument was great, but even the great warrior understood futility. They couldn't kill them all.

He'd fought, watching things he didn't understand happen around him. It was like Prometheus was in the room, or his mind was. Doors had opened and then held the enemy, giving them much-needed healing time. All kinds of things flew across the room, killing the soldiers.

There'd been no time to think, only to be grateful and continue fighting.

Caesar was bent over, hands on his knees. He looked to his left and saw the enemy also either on the floor or bent over.

Caesar had never experienced anything like that, but he knew the message's sender. Somehow her voice had been in his mind—the AllMother.

To the roof. All of you.

Pro was covering the top, and that meant he was on the roof. Caesar straightened, hooking his sabers while rushing to the humans. He picked each up with one arm, grabbing the collars of their armor, then put them on their feet.

For a creature who didn't strategize, he made a quick decision. "You won't make it on the stairs. Take the elevator. I'll keep them at bay and meet you up there."

Brillin said nothing, still in a daze.

The enemy was slowly regaining their feet. If Caesar didn't give the elevator time, these hybrids could rip through the door and get to the power line, ending any chance that they'd make it up.

Caesar took another step to the far wall and slapped the elevator's panel. There were no numbers to give the floors because the thing moved too fast. Caesar had ridden it many times over the months.

He returned to the humans, his eyes on the confused enemy. They were trying to understand what had happened and what that message meant.

Relm's faceplate drew back. "It was an honor."

"I will meet you up there," the giant growled.

The elevator door dinged and opened.

"Now *go!*" Caesar picked them up again and tossed them in. They hit the opposite wall. Relm's faceplate was still open, and a wild grin was plastered on his face. He raised his MechPulse and made a mock shot at the gigante.

The door shut.

Caesar turned.

Smart words were for Relm and Prometheus. They dealt in language.

The giant pulled the sabers off his belt, and the green lasers came to life.

Caesar dealt in blood.

He went forth again, and indeed, blood was spilled.

Prometheus stood.

The woman had courage since she didn't flee. She stood at the other end of the tunnel and pulled something Prometheus had never seen from her belt. She strapped it onto her hand, and he got a better look.

There was a black circular pad on her palm and a single strap going around the back of her hand.

She reached down to her belt again and pulled a second pad off, strapping it to the opposite hand.

"Obs, to Nero!" Pro shouted so the animal could hear him.

A few screams, then movement as the huge drathe created a path through the enemy, Thoreaux following on his heels.

The battle had stopped. Perhaps it was out of awe, or perhaps respect for their queen. Maybe it was a cultural thing with these ice people and creatures. Prometheus didn't know and didn't care.

He hooked his Whip to his belt and took off his helmet.

"You have two decisions to make, Queen. The first is, you can surrender and save your family, or you can fight and die."

"That's no choice," she called back. "My people are made from ice. We don't know how to bend the knee. The godsdamn ice is too cold."

He nodded and started retracting his armor, revealing clothing and bare skin.

He detached the leg armor, the arms, and finally the torso. He tossed it all on the roof.

"The second decision is for your people up here. I can toss them all off right now, or they can stand back and watch this fight. If they interfere at any time, every one of them falls."

The queen scanned the roof. The dead were everywhere. It was almost impossible not to stand on them. The living stared at her, waiting for her decision.

Luna's voice came next. *These people love this woman like yours do you, Allie. They'll die for her right now if she says so.*

"They won't interfere," the Ice Queen said. "My family and slaves, retreat to the edge of the roof."

Movement was immediate. Every single enemy obeyed the woman's orders without a thought.

Only the dead remained.

Prometheus knelt by his armor and pulled his Whip from the belt. He looked around at the bodies. Were they so different than his people? Those at the perimeter who had followed his orders, knowing they would most likely die? No, they weren't.

"You all deserved better," he whispered.

His mind spread across the roof. He was as gentle as he could be, moving the dead bodies, clearing the deck for this battle.

He laid them in front of their comrades. Still kneeling, he looked over his shoulder. "Obs, to me."

The drathe walked forward, his huge body higher than his master's head. "Love you, ya dumb dog. Whatever happens, keep the other two alive until this is over. None of you interfere."

Obs, unable to let the slight go, grabbed his master's shoulder. He gave it one playful bite, then bit down again. *Hard.* Prometheus gasped but didn't pull back.

The animal was covered in blood, but he brought his

head down and rubbed his master's blood first on the left side of his face, then the right. He met Pro's eyes.

"See it and die," Pro said.

He rose to his feet.

The woman in front of him clapped her hands together and the pads hardened, turning into solid discs.

The warriors stared at each other, knowing their lives were all that kept their families from being destroyed. Both were ready to die on this roof.

A thought from Alistair moved through the shared mind. *She's not so different from me.*

Prometheus shut it down. *She brought the fight here. The god who brought fire requires a tax for war. She's going to pay it.*

The Whip unfurled, its three lasers lazily twisting next to their owner's leg.

The Ice Queen moved first, beginning to circle.

Prometheus stepped forward, closing the gap. He would use none of his mind's ability on this woman. She would face only his body.

Cristin continued circling as Pro closed the gap between them.

At three meters, she attacked.

Lunging as he had to create the tunnel, she thrust both hands forward. A blue blast shot from them—not a laser, not plasma, but something entirely new. Prometheus barely had time to register the blue ball barreling toward him.

He twirled easily to his left, and the blast missed him by millimeters. He glanced to where the ball should have been, but it had dissipated.

When he looked back, another was flying toward him.

This time his spin wasn't fast enough. The blue caught his shoulder and latched on like it was alive.

The burn was immediate and excruciating.

The stuff started spreading, multiplying as it latched onto more of his skin.

Another was coming for him. Prometheus had only one choice; he fell back, dropping his Whip to grab the blue substance. He ripped it off his body and tossed it into the air, but even as he did it, the thing didn't stop trying to latch onto his hand.

It dissipated in the air, but there wasn't time to consider anything else. Two more blasts were heading toward him.

He rolled, grabbing his Whip, and watched as the blue substance turned liquid when it hit the roof next to him, burning it as it had him.

His shoulder felt like fire was still burning across it.

Prometheus reached his feet as another blast hit him, this time his leg. The fire-like pain erupted there. Pro reached down before the stuff could spread and tossed it away.

Another blast, and another.

Prometheus dodged the first and swung his Whip at the second.

The stuff latched onto the lasers, putting them out in spots.

Too much was happening for him to even look at the woman or where she was moving. He killed the Whip, immediately bringing it back to life. The lasers were normal, the blue substance gone.

His mind kept calculating even as his body reacted to the never-ending shots. Another hit his right arm, and another his left calf. His body was now that of a burn victim, and he couldn't close the gap.

The elevator door opened, and that was the only respite from the onslaught. The Ice Queen looked over her shoulder as Prometheus saw who was there.

Brillin's and Relm's faces were masks of terror as they looked at their leader.

Cristin turned to him again, and one more door opened. Servia stepped onto the roof, the AllMother leaning heavily on her shoulder.

The Ice Queen found Pro's eyes and smiled. "Is this all of your family?"

Despite the pain, he knew Caesar wasn't here. "There's one more inside."

The Ice Queen spoke softly to the comm in her ear. A moment passed with no one moving. Pro took a look at Servia, and she looked more frightened than Relm. The AllMother's lids were heavy, her face slack.

"They're bringing him, too," Cristin called from a few meters away. "They can all watch you die. I think you'll die a good death, Kane, and it's something they should see. You're not a bad leader. You just lack the coldness this universe demands."

The woman had honor. Despite him being on the ropes, she'd give him this break for Caesar to get up here, though Pro had no idea what it meant that "they" were bringing him.

He took a knee and looked at his body. It was easy to understand his friend's faces. His skin was savaged, muscles visible across much of his body. Even those were blackened from the burns.

The elevator opened on the other side of the roof. Two hybrids tossed Caesar on the roof, then stepped to the side. He hit it hard and didn't even try to hold himself up. Nanotech was crawling almost drunkenly over the giant's body. The gigante was still breathing, though shallowly. His eyes were open, and he stared at his burned leader.

Relm knelt by his side. He tried to raise the gigante, but Caesar fell back to the roof.

Prometheus saw the corvette behind the Ice Queen. Faitrin was here too.

Four light beams came from the corners of the building, and a massive holovid appeared above them. It was ten times the size of those it showed. No one in the city could miss it.

Jeeves understood. That was his work, and he knew it came down to this.

The Ice Queen looked up curiously, then shrugged.

She put her focus back on Pro.

"You're a warrior. Now die as one," the bitch said. She lunged forward once more and shot her blast. Prometheus didn't move at first. His eyes took in everything, and his mind analyzed it. He could not just react here. He could not brazenly rely on his skills.

At the last moment, he moved, twisting on one knee. The blast dissipated behind him. He returned to his kneeling position as the next blast came. Again, he watched and moved. And again. And again.

He was fast enough to dodge these blasts, but he had to remain aware.

Prometheus rose. The beautiful specimen was gone, over thirty percent of his body badly burned. He felt his strength slowly ebbing, but he forced that down. The blasts kept coming, but he slowly worked his way forward. He spun here and turned there, always returning to look at his attacker.

Each blast missed.

Each step brought him closer.

The woman's face was granite. No fear. No desire. Just the cool touch of iced-over rock.

Two meters out, he knew he was too close to dodge any longer and unfurled his Whip. He slashed through the next blast and killed the Whip, then brought it back to life. It was *just* fast enough to catch the next one. Again, the lasers were killed by the blue, and again they came back to life.

At one meter, the Ice Queen came forward. She was faster than any woman he'd ever seen, easily as fast as a man. His own ravaged body was slow. The discs were now bright blue, and her hands were so quick there appeared to be four of them.

She slapped his ribs three times, then bounced back. The substance was on him, though less. It started its spread.

No time to pull them off.

The time for observation was at an end.

She pounced again, but this time he met her. He wasn't fast enough to get his Whip across her body.

A single, clear thought went through his mind. *Fuck it.*

He dropped the Whip and grabbed her bicep. She clamped down with her discs on his arms. Prometheus raised the woman into the air, his damaged muscles bulging against nonexistent flesh. He spun, gained momentum, and slammed her into the roof.

It cracked.

Her hands were vipers. They didn't stop, delivering light slaps that allowed her to pull back and hit again much faster than any punch.

The blue was spreading.

Prometheus raised his right hand into the air as she slapped his face.

The fist fell. Facial muscles cracked.

The slaps kept coming, the blue almost covering him now. His fists rained down on her face.

It took five blows, but in the end, bone entered her brain. Her hands fell away as her pupils dilated. Prometheus stared at her for a moment, then slumped to the side, his body almost completely blue.

No one moved.

No one said a word.

Obs finally broke the stillness. He was the only sign that Pro still lived because he did.

He gave a loud yelp and bolted forward, getting to his master in seconds.

The drathe gently rolled Prometheus off the dead woman. The blue latched onto his nose and began its path of destruction, but the drathe didn't move. His whimpers had nothing to do with his pain.

The giant holovid showed it all.

A low sound grew louder, increasing second by second. It started as a whisper of wind and within five seconds was the buzzing of a thousand beehives.

The nanotech rolled up the side of the building and curled over the top of the roof. It ran over foe and friend alike, heading toward the two people lying in the middle.

Caesar stretched his hand out, the skin opening, and a trickle of mechanical insects came from his arm. Nero stood, putting all his weight on his left leg. He opened both hands, and his nanotech met the rolling wave.

The insects covered both bodies, even going into the woman's mouth.

After a long minute, the nanotech lifted off the woman and moved to the man.

His eyes, his mouth, his nose—every centimeter was covered with them.

A small group found Obs and began healing him. The drathe growled and tried to shake them off, but they wouldn't leave. He only wanted to look at his master.

Finally, the wave was done, every single one of them on the man who'd freed a planet.

Minutes that felt like hours passed with no one moving. No one spoke.

Finally, the insects started to disintegrate. Those on top fell off, then the next layer, and so on until only a naked man remained.

His eyes were open and his chest moved, but nothing else did.

Obs laid down next to his ribs, the insects on his snout gone. He rested his head on his master's shoulder and lightly licked his face.

The shout came from below first. It was frail. Soft.

Then it came again, a little louder.

The noise spread to others. No one on the roof could understand it, just heard the noise.

Thoreaux stepped forward. He was the first to understand. The noise was growing louder, moving up the side of the skyscraper like the nanotech had.

"*Ave*, Prometheus!" he shouted.

It came again, and this time the words could be understood.

Thoreaux shouted in unison with them. "*Ave*, Prometheus!"

The next one roared like thunder over a prairie. Thoreaux looked across the roof, finally realizing what the man in the middle had done. His mind saw it all clearly, even as his mouth shouted the words. This roar wasn't only from the gigantes below. It wasn't only from the AllMother's children. The fucking *hybrids* were screaming.

Everyone somehow united by what they'd just seen.

Ave, Prometheus.

THE WRITTEN HISTORY OF THE GREAT INSURRECTION

After that victory, other things took place. The hunting of the remaining warlords, the few and short battles with those who wouldn't join us, and a couple of other matters.

I want to take a few pages to discuss what happened on that roof and below first, though. I'll get to the rest later.

I haven't been alive for very long, not compared to some of those involved in this insurrection. I have not yet reached the end of Prometheus' story. Indeed, I'm still living it as I write these entries. Perhaps the end will change things...

As of now, though, I've never seen anything as confounding, moving, and inexplicable as what happened on that roof.

I asked Prometheus why he hadn't simply used his mental abilities to defeat the woman. He didn't look at me as he responded but stared into the distance as if trying to see the Ice Queen again.

"She deserved a fair fight," he told me.

I think, though he's never said it, that he respected the

woman. I think Pro comes to understand his enemies in a way I will never be able to. I think he hated her but also respected her.

The shouts supporting Prometheus were... Even as I write about this, I get chills. How did he do that? How did he change a war with one fight?

I've had the chance to speak to the hybrids and humans who fought for the Ice Queen, and I suppose I'll write down what they told me as much for myself as for those who read this later. For me to fully understand it, I need to explain it concretely.

Jeeves, the artificial intelligence, should be credited for almost all of it. Had the battle not been broadcast so high in the air, none of the following would have occurred. He also put the fight on every screen in every room across the city. Everyone saw what happened. If he hadn't done that, the chanting wouldn't have started. The enemy had to see Prometheus defeat her, and that was something he hadn't thought about.

That was Jeeves' genius. His insight changed so much.

Their willingness to scream those words after watching their queen die partly has to do with their culture. The place they came from, which I eventually saw with my own eyes, was a world unlike any other I've come across. How it developed, I'm still not certain. Once a world covered in water, it was now a rock covered in ice. In that cold, desolate place, the need to follow a strong leader must have been paramount throughout their evolution. To not follow someone who knew what they were doing would have meant certain death.

Thus, seeing their leader fall to someone like

Prometheus…to not follow him might have meant certain death in some part of their minds.

I think culture had something to do with it.

Their Ice Queen did too.

I looked into her history. She made her bones in the ten-year war with the other warlords, and she was a deadly adversary. After studying her and talking to her former soldiers, I realized she would have never simply squared off against someone like that. Cristin de Monaham would have considered most opponents beneath her and killed them immediately or deemed them not worth her time.

To those that followed her, she'd *honored* Prometheus by fighting him.

Allowing those he loved to see his last fight? A great honor.

In her way, the Ice Queen had set him up as someone to be respected.

Other things come into play—the demoralization of their army, the new hope of our own. Perhaps the enemy understood the tide was going to change and they were going to die? No one ever told me that, but it probably played a part.

All those things were important for Prometheus to gain a larger army, but I think in the end, it came down to him.

Prometheus, Alistair Kane, is a uniter of people. I said at the beginning of chronicling this endeavor that I would follow him anywhere. Nearly everyone I love would do the same. The man brings people to him, then propels those people forward.

To watch what he did against a warrior like the Ice Queen? To watch a species freed because of him save his life? It would have been hard for anyone not to want to follow him. He was beaten. I saw it. Servia saw it. Everyone saw it. He was dying on his feet. Only willpower carried him through, and I think those watching knew that.

In the end, I can list the reasons I think Prometheus is capable of doing the things he does, but even knowing those reasons, *I* can't do it.

Only he can.

In the end, Prometheus is the reason—the reason I follow. The reason this insurrection is heading back to Earth for a final confrontation. The reason for all of this.

I can't know for certain how he united those people with ours. I can't know for certain how he does what he does.

I can only be thankful for it.

The story continues with *Prometheus Ascends* available at Amazon and through Kindle Unlimited.

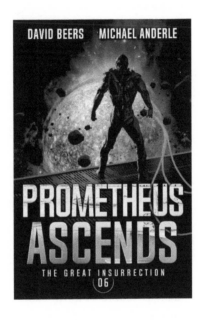

Claim your copy today!

The Great Insurrection Series is also available in audio. The series is available as unabridged audiobooks narrated by the talented John Skelley.

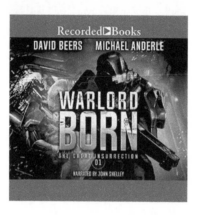

Start the series on Audio!

The series is also available as a full cast audio recording with cinematic sound effects from Graphic Audio.

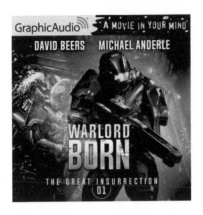

Start the Dramatized Version today from Graphic Audio!

I didn't know where this note was going when I started—just sorta free wrote. Turns out, this is an Ode to Alistair Kane (without the poetry or talent of Greek poets, go figure). Now, given that I'm the author of this series, it may seem it's an ode to me. Trust me, that's not the case. I can't explain it any better than this, but I don't create or direct any of my characters. I give them space, then they show me who they are. My job here is to give them space, then sit down at the computer long enough to write out what they show me. That's it. I'm merely dictation to these folks. Without further ado, let me sing of my love to Alistair —LOL.

The Dark Tower by Stephen King is in my top three favorite series. I like badasses, but I don't want them to be *too* badass. I need to think they can die. As a kid, I couldn't play video games on god mode. It was just too boring, and that's the way I feel about fictional characters (don't get me started on Superman, and if you're a fan of his, don't email me to curse me out either).

The main character in The Dark Tower, Roland Deschain, is just that type of a character. He's a badass, but he's not unstoppable.

The other thing I need is growth. A static character that doesn't learn anything...Well, it's a bit too much like some of the people I see in real life (I know you know who I'm talking about). They repeat the same mistakes over and over. That movie gets old quick, but growth? Now, growth is something I can get behind.

Roland Deschain grows throughout The Dark Tower, turning into almost a different man by the end.

As a writer, I write what I'd want to read, and I think I'm achieving it. That's not to say I'm in the realm of Stephen King, but I know when writing this book, I wasn't even sure how Alistair would get himself out of the obstacles thrown at him. That corvette crash? I didn't see it coming until you did, which is when it happened.

I almost cursed Alistair. Seriously. Like, "FUCK, MAN! I can't have you die in book five when there are four more to write. Figure out how to live, because you're really messing things up right now."

A malleable mind is an important thing, and I love the way Alistair changes as this series progresses. He moves from a Subversive killer, to wielding their war banner. Alistair isn't necessarily stubborn; he'll listen. He just needs to be punched in the mouth first. I like both of those things, because it's a man who believes in himself, but eventually, recognizes his own limitations.

Let the AllSeer consider himself godlike. I want my heroes knowing they can be better...and working toward it.

However, despite all that growth, Alistair's goal hasn't changed. He's going home. He's going to his wife. Perhaps that why I like him most. On the surface, this is a science fiction series. A space opera. At its core? This is a love story. Maybe I'm a hopeless romantic, but tell me that you wouldn't swoon for someone willing to burn worlds and fight across galaxies just to see you one last time?

We all would.

Don't tell Mike that hopeless romantic stuff. Or Steve. I've got a reputation around LMBPN, and it must be kept intact.

All the best,
db

AUTHOR NOTES - MICHAEL ANDERLE
AUGUST 4, 2021

Thank you for not only reading this hopelessly romantic love story—sorry, space opera—but these author notes in the back as well.

(Did you see how I didn't mention anything about Steve reading those last lines yet?)

I am going to touch on the following quote from David in my author notes:

I almost cursed Alistair. Seriously. Like, "FUCK, MAN! I can't have you die in book five when there are four more to write. Figure out how to live because you're really messing things up right now."

I believe most authors will resonate with this comment. When the characters are their own people, the human brain has this wonderful ability to inhabit other personalities simultaneously.

Fortunately for us authors, they don't stick us in the mental ward for this trait. Given enough fans, society actually applauds our ability to have multiple personalities. I have no idea how close we authors are to allowing this to become a problem, but there are plenty of examples in history where authors didn't clamp down on this talent well enough.

My most grievous example has nothing to do with dying a few books short of the end (seriously, David? NOW you tell me this?)

Rather, compared to David's, my story is rather lame.

At the end of one of the Kurtherian Gambit books, a main character is going to propose marriage to a lady in the next book. At the end of the book I was working on, he starts to get down on one knee, and as I am typing this, I'm having that feeling of "What the *HELL* are you doing? This wasn't where you were supposed to ask her to marry you. This is in the middle of a damned military base air hanger!"

Fortunately for me, the lady said yes. I've no idea what I would have done as the author had she decided she didn't want the ring.

Actually, I do, *and this is the scary part*: I would have had a three-way discussion with the two characters in my head.

See, multiple personality disorder!

Considering the hundreds of stories I've been part of and the massive number of characters I have created, I am a bit worried about myself. If you ever meet me and I am talking to myself, just stick a laptop in front of me.

(*Editor's note: Agree. It doesn't even have to be turned on or functional. It makes him happy and calm. Trust me!*)

I feel confident the voices will go away eventually.

See you next book!

Ad Aeternitatem,
Michael Anderle

ALSO BY DAVID BEERS

Nemesis

She's coming and no one can stop her...

An alien Queen, Morena, was removed from power and forced into exile. Doomed to roam space forever, with no hope of return.

Until a random party brings a man named Michael to her crashed ship. For the first time in millennia, Morena sees her salvation. First, in Michael … and then Earth. The perfect place to repopulate her species. And those already here? **They can bow or die.**

As Morena begins her conquest, can Michael warn the world before it's too late? Can anyone stop the most powerful force the world has ever seen?

Earth's final Nemesis has arrived.

265

Don't miss this pulse-pounding science fiction series! If you love thought provoking thrill-rides, grab this book today!

The Singularity

One thousand years in the future, humans no longer rule...

In the early twenty-first century, humanity marveled at its greatest creation: Artificial Intelligence. They never foresaw the consequences of such a creation, though...

Now, in a world where humans must meet specifications to continue living, a man named Caesar emerges. Different, both in thought and talent, Caesar somehow slipped through the genetic net meant to catch those like him.

Eyes are falling on Caesar now, though, and he can no longer hide. The Artificial Intelligence wants him dead, but others want him to lead their revolution...

Can one man stand against humanity's greatest creation? A don't-miss epic science fiction novel that pits one man fighting for the future of all people!

Red Rain

What would you do if you couldn't stop killing?

John Hilt lives The American Dream. His corner office looks out on Dallas's beautiful skyline. His amazing wife and children love him. His father and sister adore him. John has it all.

Except every few years, when Harry shows back up. Harry wants John to kill people. Harry wants to watch the world burn.

Murderous thoughts take hold of John, and as flames ignite across his life, the sky doesn't send cool rain water, but blood to feed their hunger.

If you love taut, psychological thrillers, grab Red Rain today and prepare to sleep with the lights on!

The Devil's Dream

He'll raise the dead, at all costs...

Perhaps the smartest man to ever live, Matthew Brand changed the world by twenty-five years old. In his mid-thirties, he still shaped the world as he wanted, until cops gunned down his son on the street.

Brand's life changed then. He forgot about bettering Earth and started trying to resurrect his son.

Eventually, Brand's mind overpowered even death's mysteries; he discovered how to bring back the dead--he only needed living bodies to make his son's life possible again. Why not use the bodies of those who killed his son? In the largest manhunt the FBI's ever experienced, how do they stop a man who can calculate all the odds and stack them in his favor?

CONNECT WITH THE AUTHORS

Connect with David and sign up for his email list here:

Email list
http://www.davidbeersauthor.com/mailing-list

Website
http://www.davidbeersfiction.com/

Social Media:

https://www.facebook.com/davidbeersauthor

Email List: http://lmbpn.com/email/

Connect with Michael and sign up for his email list here:

Website: http://lmbpn.com

Email List: http://lmbpn.com/email/

Social Media:

https://www.facebook.com/LMBPNPublishing

https://twitter.com/MichaelAnderle

https://www.instagram.com/lmbpn_publishing/

https://www.bookbub.com/authors/michael-anderle

Ingram Content Group UK Ltd.
Milton Keynes UK
UKHW010019070423
419773UK00005B/571